CW00548603

Thunderbolt's Last Run

Thomas F Young

With illustrations by John Wardle

Inspired by T.E.B. Clarke's The Titfield Thunderbolt.

Thunderbolt Books
Bath
2022

Copyright Thomas Frederick Young

All rights reserved. No part of this publication may be reproduced, stored in a retrieval system, or transmitted in any form or by any means, electronic, mechanical, photocopying, recording or otherwise without the permission of the publisher.

Published by Thunderbolt Books

An imprint of Wild Swan Books

4 Tollbridge Studios
Toll Bridge Road
Batheaston
Bath
BA1 7DE

ISBN 9781912038275

Copyright Notice

Thomas Young asserts his right under the Copyright, Designs and Patents Act 1988 to be identified as the author of his work.

Designed and typeset by Rich Carter | www.richcstudio.co.uk
Typeset in Garamond Pro and Proxima Nova
Cover images courtesy of StudioCanal
Book illustrations by John Wardle

Printed in Great Britain by Short Run Press, Exeter.

For my marvellous Wife Betty, Shaun, Keith, Dawn and Kay:
now make an old man happy and read it.

—

Foreword

—

Tom first saw "The Titfield Thunderbolt" at South Shields Odeon in the summer of 1953 as a 16 year old apprentice motor mechanic, falling in love with an old locomotive and a slightly less old barmaid in the process.

National Service and a growing family followed, with Tom working his way up from machine operator to training manager within the Bunzl organisation before later joining the Prison Service from which he retired in 1999.

Tom never lost his affection for Titfield and its characters, and apart from occasional airings on the television he acquired his own copy of the film when a National newspaper gave away DVDs of this and other classic British films in the 1990s.

Seeing, and then purchasing, a small book on the subject in the "Midland Counties" list a few years later, Tom found that the film had been made near Bath and with a visit to the area in mind, he contacted the book's author.

Which is how the two of us met, and shortly afterwards I had the great pleasure of showing Tom and his wife Betty around the countryside south of Bath in which the film had been made in the summer of 1952, accompanied by my then young son Harry.

Sharing thoughts about the film in the sunshine over a drink at the "Wheelwrights" in Monkton Combe (where the film's cast and crew had certainly shared a "mild and bitter" or two) our thoughts turned to what would have happened to the villagers of Titfield and their railway after the events depicted in the film.

Tom explained that there were certainly a few "issues" from a judicial point of view at the end of the film, and in common with other fans we were both slightly troubled by the "stolen locomotive" sequence – although we tried not to talk about it too much(!) Our conversation set us thinking though, and we parted with Tom pondering just what might have "happened next".

A lasting friendship resulted from this happy meeting and some while later Tom phoned to tell me that he had decided to set down on paper what had actually happened to the villagers of Titfield and their railway, all those years ago.

The result is the book you are now holding, a completely original piece of writing by Tom that takes the scenes and characters created by the film's writer "Tibby" Clarke back in 1951, and through imagination, new characters and good storytelling finishes the tale off in a most satisfying and pleasing of ways.

As an aside, I think the BBC may have had a hand in this magic as many years ago Tom (while working at Bunzl) managed to get himself enrolled on to one of the BBC's prestigious residential training courses at Wood Norton near Evesham. Despite masking a complete lack of all the required qualifications for admission, Tom nevertheless successfully completed the course that covered editing, lighting, sound and vision - even managing, for the first time, to get his hands on to a mixing desk!

Apart from his warmth, wit and skill for telling stories, Tom has a link to the original film that very few people can claim. In 1949, as a 12 year old boy, Tom actually visited and travelled upon the Talyllyn Railway before it became the World's first preserved railway and two years before Tibby Clarke visited the line and got the idea that led to his writing "The Titfield Thunderbolt".

As you might by now expect, this was a story in itself, with Tom and his Mam Emily Jane somehow managing to travel all the way from County Durham to Tonfanu, just south of Towyn, on a specially ordered troop train. They there joined Tom's father Thomas Henry for a few days holiday before returning. Having served in Burma during the War his father, like many other servicemen at the time, had gone into the Territorial Army and was at the time undergoing training at Tonfanu camp. His work outside the Army was in mining, he later returned to coal mining, becoming a deputy overman.

As Tom recalls, their journey on the Talyllyn was as far as Dolgoch where they visited the famous falls. Included in this whole adventure were family friends Norman and Maudy Mountain, who had also made the long journey from County Durham to Wales and return by troop train - and as Tom recounts the whole thing didn't cost them a penny!

So, seventy years later, travel back with me to Titfield, and let Tom tell us what happened after that night of celebration in the "Grasshopper"....

Simon Castens

Chapters

—

The Titfield Thunderbolt Characters

The Reverend Sam Weech	*Vicar of Titfield*
Mr Gordon Chesterford	*Squire of Titfield*
Mr Walter Valentine	*Retired City Broker*
Dan Taylor	*Retired Plate Layer*
Harry Hawkins	*Steam Roller Driver/Owner*
Mr Blakeworth	*Mallingford Town Clerk*
Bishop Oliver Matthews	*Bishop of Wellchester*
Emily	*Reverend Weech's Housekeeper*
Fred Hampton	*Landlord of the Grasshopper Pub*
Joan Hampton	*Daughter of Fred, and Barmaid*
Seth	*Retired Handyman*
William	*Station Helper*
Mr Ruddock	*Ministry of Transport*
Mr Clegg	*Ministry of Transport*
Vernon Crump	*Owner of Bus Company*
Alec Pearce	*Owner of Bus Company*

New Characters

Taff Jenkins	*Signalman at Mallingford*
Ernie	*Booking boy*
Mrs Felicity Valentine	*Wife of Mr. Valentine*
Alistair	*First brother of Alec Pearce*
Fergal	*Second brother*
Frazer	*Third brother*
Ron	*Part-time help for Gordon*
Sally	*Part-time help for Emily*
Arthur Grout	*Owner of locomotive 1462*
Doris Grout	*Wife of above*
Albert Lee	*Retired Railway Engineer*
Sandy	*School kid with four friends*
Dick Bird (Dickey)	*Traction engine owner driver*
Ron Foskit (Fossy)	*Traction engine owner driver*
Joe Bombswith (Bomb)	*Traction engine owner driver*

PROLOGUE

Tuesday evening

—

Celebration

The noise of raucous celebrations were still coming from the "Grasshopper" as the Reverend Weech closed the door and stepped out into the warm evening air. It had been a momentous day for the railway in getting Ministry permission to carry on, everyone was entitled to a good celebration after all the challenges they had faced.

He walked up the hill towards the Vicarage, enjoying the clear night air as he passed the Valentine's house, its windows unusually dark as Walter and Felicity Valentine were both in the "Grasshopper" celebrating success.

But we have been lucky, he thought. It was a serious offence to steal a locomotive and the list of charges had been impressive, but thankfully Mr Valentine's good standing and the popularity of the railway had seen the Magistrate let both him and Dan go free with just a fine. Pearce and Crump's offence had been too serious for the Magistrate to deal with and they had both been remanded to Prison to await judge and jury and the Crown Court.

Pearce and Crump still worried him, they ran the bus company which was the railway's only rival and would not be at all happy with the situation, could they cause the railway further problems – even from Prison?

And then there was the matter of suitable rolling stock, they needed to run an efficient service with a modern locomotive and coach. Their train had been wrecked by Pearce and Crump and *Thunderbolt* was only borrowed from the museum. New stock was desperately needed, but where was the money to be found?

He was deep in thought as he reached the Churchyard and went through to the Vicarage, the hall light thoughtfully left on for him by his housekeeper

Emily. As he got into bed thoughts crowded into his head. How could the railway survive without proper stock, where would they find more staff to keep the railway running and could they survive any more trouble from Pearce and Crump?

CHAPTER 1

Wednesday

—

Recruitment

The main line express headed by a green West Country Class pacific thundered across the viaduct as *Thunderbolt* and its train emerged along the branch line beneath it, the Reverend Weech giving a toot on the old locomotive's whistle as they headed back towards Titfield on the last run of the day.

Dan steadied himself as he bent low to bring his shovel sliding across the footplate and out of the tender, shooting the contents through the fire door and closing it with the back of the shovel blade. He looked across the valley and at the gathering black clouds, "We are going to get wet Reverend" he said in his low Welsh growl, the words being most of the few he had uttered all day.

"Indeed Dan, indeed." The Reverend Weech looked over the rim of the tender. "You know Dan; I have no sympathy with you, drinking with Mr Valentine until all hours. He will no doubt be recovering whilst you have to work – you are not getting any younger you know Dan".

Dan turned his back on the Vicar and his scolding with a grunt. Reverend Weech glanced up at the rapidly gathering dark clouds and fastened his overall jacket buttons. "It is a pity we have not got any waterproofs Dan" – now he could see the rain sweeping towards them.

He tried to get more speed out of the old girl, they still had to climb the gradient and Dan muttered an oath as the first raindrops hit home, stinging his exposed hands and face. The valley which had been so green, bright and sunny on their last run now seemed to hold the bleakness of mid-winter. Within a few minutes they were soaked through and cold was eating into them. Black slurry was washing across the footplate from the tender making

it even more difficult to keep their balance on the swaying engine. Spits of steam were coming off the fire door as the rain hit it, Dan was standing sideways against the oncoming rain to keep feeding the firebox, and the fire bed was sending showers of ash back at him as the wet coal hit. "Ruddy rain" growled Dan, scowling at the steam pressure gauge.

"Still, you are free Dan, it could have gone against you." Reverend Weech hunched his shoulders, trying to avoid the rain going down the back of his neck.

"Why, for trying to right a wrong?" Dan felt hurt that anyone could doubt that his actions were not of the highest order.

"You took an engine Dan" Reverend Weech tried to sound sympathetic.

"That is all, and old Valentine was with me all the way."

"But Dan it was stealing," sighed the Reverend, "and the damage."

"What damage? We didn't damage that engine by bumping it into a tree!" Dan's singsong Welsh voice was rising.

"There was the fence you went through, and the Mallingford road sign – you were really very, very lucky."

Thunderbolt swayed and rocked as her motion moved faster, chuffing on with steam thrashing and smoke bellowing out of her tall chimney. The rain was not easing and their bodies were still taking the full force of the weather without any protection.

Dan finished another hard spell of stoking and put his shovel in the tender, black slurry running across the footplate and being carried out and down the tender wheels by the slipstream. "At least we fared better than Pearce and Crump – sent them down he did," Dan gave the Reverend one of his wicked smiles "remanded them," he chuckled "Good job the Magistrate was an old friend of Valentine's!"

"As I said before Dan it was very fortunate" The Reverend squinted at Dan through the driving rain.

"There was nothing fortunate about it Reverend" said Dan. "Old Valentine said he would pay for any damage done and give a generous donation to the police benevolent fund too. That sergeant's face split in two with a smile, he gave a nod and we got a fine." He hung onto the side of the tender and roared with laughter, the raindrops shaking off his cap.

"Fortunate." The Rev allowed himself a wry smile. "Water tower coming up – not long to go now."

"Where's your mate, the Bishop?" Dan tried to get some life back into his pipe.

"He was helping me with the firing whilst you were celebrating, but decided to go back to Wellchester. He could have remained though and you would have been out of a job".

Dan scowled at him "On a day like this he could have it."

They drew on to the level track approaching Titfield Station and the Reverend Weech closed the regulator, the train stopping opposite the booking office door.

Emily was standing in the doorway and behind her a fire was lit, the room beyond warm and inviting. "Mr Weech come in quickly out of the rain." Emily opened the door wide as they came off the engine, squelching across the flagstones. "Quickly now, get out of those wet things." She had large towels waiting, but hesitated before handing one to Dan, who gave her one of his glowering looks.

The Reverend and Dan sat on chairs in front of the fire, warming themselves and rubbing their wet hair dry, in Dan's case with the towel getting dirtier as he rubbed.

The Squire rushed in from the Platform whilst the passengers came out of Dan's coach, moving off quite cheerfully into the rain and admiring *Thunderbolt* as they passed by.

"I am so sorry Sam, there was nothing I could do – I felt such a fraud staying so dry in the brake van." "Ah well, one of the disadvantages of our temporary motive power I am afraid" replied the Reverend, "it won't be a problem when we get our modern locomotive back."

Dan was down to his vest and with the towel completely covering his head when Mr Valentine came in through the door, removing his Trilby with his usual flourish. "I say, I say, a wonderful run – she got quite a speed up. Definitely shook the generals, Oh Padre, I am so sorry, how remiss of me – you must have got soaked".

Dan turned away from the fire to face Valentine and pulled the towel from his head. "There are two of us on that ruddy footplate you know!".

"Dan, Dan, my good fellow; I did not mean to imply you were any less important, we share a great bond – we have been in the jaws of adversity together". He went across to Dan and offered him his hip flask; Dan quickly took it and swigged the contents, finishing by wiping the back of his hand across his mouth and giving a loud belch. Emily gave him a despairing glare as she produced steaming mugs of tea for the men, Mr Valentine politely refusing the offered mug.

After finishing his tea, the Reverend Weech retired to the booking office to change his clothes. Dan picked up the bundle which Emily had placed by his chair. "Here, these are my best things – I can't go messing about on engines in my best things!" he said, his voice rising with indignation. The Reverend put his head around the doorway. "Look, we will sort you out with some new things Dan. In the meantime Emily has brought some oilskins which you can put on over your clothes – we have got to get *Thunderbolt* back into the shed."

"Alright then, just so long as I am not out of pocket." Dan scowled at poor Emily.

Mr Valentine unfurled his smart umbrella. "Must be getting on my way or my dear wife will be wondering where I have got to – I will see you all later in the Grasshopper." With that he was gone.

A lot drier and warmer, Reverend Weech and Dan climbed back aboard the footplate while the Squire climbed down behind the tender to uncouple, so that *Thunderbolt* could run around its train. This completed, the Reverend Weech eased the old locomotive up against the train and shunted it back under the Dutch barn, *Thunderbolt*'s shed. "We will drop the fire and give her a clean and then we are done." The fire was dropped, red hot embers fizzing as they hit the wet ground and the firebox was raked out while the Squire joined them on the footplate and swept out the slurry down and on to the track.

As Dan followed the Reverend Weech and Squire Gordon down from the engine and on to the track he sighed, "You know we are getting a bit old for this – we need some new blood".

"I think you are quite right Dan," agreed Reverend Weech, "I must admit I have my aches and pains and we are none of us getting any younger." The three men crossed the level crossing; closing the gates back after them and turning towards the village followed the path the passengers had taken. "By the way Dan, how did you happen to be sleeping on the platform bench this morning?" The rain had stopped and he opened his oilskin jacket to get a little cooler.

Dan tried to sort out his hazy memory. "Can't rightly say Reverend, but I know I haven't slept in a proper bed these past two nights."

Gordon looked up "Good grief Dan – we must find you a place to stay." He turned to the Reverend Weech. "What do you think Sam?"

Dan butted in – he was going to get things off his chest. "I have got my own place and that is where I will be sleeping tonight!" He gestured with his left thumb, jabbing it over his shoulder towards the engine shed and the train.

"But there is no bed" Gordon protested.

"Then I will use the sofa, but only temporary mind – I need my own bed!" retorted Dan.

"Alright, we will see what we can do," promised the Reverend, "I suppose you are off to the pub now?" he already knew the coming reply.

"You're darn right I am, I've got my best suit on under this lot – see you later." Dan gave a slight wave and turned and walked off in the direction of the pub, they watched him go.

"You know Gordon, Dan is right – we need someone else." Reverend Weech put his hand on the Squire's shoulder. "Come to tea Gordon, Emily will have it ready by now and we can talk."

They went to the back porch and took off the oilskins and boots before entering. In no time they were sitting at the white clothed table with the delicate china set out for tea, the sun lighting up the room.

"You are right Sam, we need more help, but we have not got any time to train someone, we need someone right now – someone who knows steam."

The Reverend looked towards Gordon slowly shaking his head as he picked up his cup. Gradually moving it up to his lips he took a sip and suddenly his eyes opened wide and the cup went back onto the saucer with a clink. "Hawkins, Harry Hawkins" the words came carefully from his lips as he looked at Gordon, as if not really understanding what he had just said.

Both Gordon's hands banged the table at the same time making the cups rattle. "Sam, Sam you are a genius. Of course Hawkins – there is not that much difference between his roller and our engine, well done!" he leant over and patted the Reverend Weech on his shoulder.

"But what if he says no?" He looked up from the scone on his plate to Gordon.

"I think he will have to say yes Sam" Gordon leant towards The Reverend. "Mr Blakeworth said he heard Hawkins' steam roller heading towards the railway on Monday night – that was why he went to investigate. He remembers seeing steam and then the engine and carriage started to move – it would have to be something powerful to do that – Harry Hawkins must have been in it with Pearce and Crump!"

"But Gordon, how can we be sure?" Reverend Weech got up from the table to stand at the tall window overlooking the garden, as Gordon eased his chair away from the table.

"I'm right Sam, I know I am! Look; he has been trying to get Joan to marry him for ages, now he is like a dog with two tails, what with Joan agreeing to marry him and him being a hero lending us his chain."

"That is all fine and well Gordon but how does that help us?"

"Sam, all we have to suggest is that we think he might have been involved in the wreck and Joan would drop him like a hot brick – she loves the railway as much as we do!"

"That could be construed as blackmail Gordon…" Reverend Weech slowly shook his head.

"Look Sam, he could act as fireman and would be up to standard in no time at all and you said yourself you could be on the carpet for spending too much time on the Railway. We can train someone else to be a guard and to run the station, in fact we must, but to train a driver would take at least a year."

"I still have my misgivings about this Gordon…" The Reverend glanced at the clock on the mantelpiece "I think the Grasshopper will be open now…"

Mr Valentine was holding court as usual, standing every one drinks, with Dan his recent partner in crime standing close by. "The Reverend and the Squire, Mr Weech and Mr Chesterford, welcome. Inn keeper – a glass of your finest for my friends, especially after their dreadful day on the railway today."

Harry Hawkins was standing on the right hand side of the bar in front of the TV which was switched off. He looked at Reverend Weech and Squire, not knowing whether to smile a greeting or not. He looked across to Joan and she smiled back at him. The Squire and Reverend Weech chatted to Mr Valentine and some of the villagers for a while before Gordon eased himself towards the bar and Harry Hawkins. "I wonder if Mr Weech and I could have a word with you Harry".

"And what would that be about then Squire?" Harry was leaning against the counter while Joan smiled at them both from the other side of the bar.

Gordon moved closer and lowered his voice, "why don't we go into the Public Bar – I don't think Joan would like to hear what we have to say." He smiled across the bar at Joan as Harry straightened up quickly, blinking his eyes, his brain in turmoil. Gordon moved away, tapping Sam on the shoulder as he squeezed by towards the public bar, Harry following in a daze; whilst the Vicar excused himself and followed too.

They sat down at the same table where Pearce and Crump had planned their attack on the railway with Hawkins a few days before. Joan came from behind the counter with a pint of mild and bitter for Gordon, sweet sherry for the Reverend Weech and a pint of bitter for Harry – she was so happy that all her favourite men were talking together.

"Cheers!" Gordon raised his glass, and looked across at Harry. "How about coming to work on the Railway Harry, as a fireman/driver?"

"Too much on." Harry sipped his beer.

"Not full-time Harry, say a couple of weeks full time, then maybe half a week to give Mr Weech and Dan a breather – what do you say?"

Harry was just about to reply when Gordon cut in. "I bet Joan would be pleased – you know how she loves the Railway."

"But I have jobs to do…" Harry felt cornered, but he wasn't sure why.

"Think of it Harry, think how proud Joan would be – you as Engine Driver and she in charge of a Buffet Car – not Dan's old place and *Thunderbolt* mind you, we should be getting another 1400 tank and more rolling stock before too long." Harry stayed silent. Sam Weech looked at Harry, raised his eyes heaven wards then looked across at Gordon and nodded.

"You were out with your Roller on Monday Night Harry, Mr Blakeworth saw you passing his house going towards the Station. He followed you down to the station where he saw steam, which of course wasn't coming from our Engine, just before the Engine moved off. Only a Steam Roller or Traction Engine would have had the power to move our Train. Harry; Pearce and Crump are on remand – maybe you'd like to join them?"

"Now wait a minute, wait a minute!" Harry was spluttering desperately, thinking how he could get out of this situation.

"We don't have to wait Harry, we don't have to go to the Police – all we have to do is get up from this table now and tell Joan of our suspicions. And of course Mr Blakeworth could tell her what he saw" Gordon added as he turned in his seat and looked across the room towards Joan. Joan beamed back at them and Harry's heart raised and sank. He gulped down the rest of his pint, sweat was breaking out on his brow as he rubbed his sweating palms on his Army battle dress work trousers.

"We don't want to know your reasons for doing what you did Harry, I am sure we can find it in our hearts to forgive you". The Reverend Weech had decided to make his contribution. "If you agree to join us this would be a fresh start and of course Joan would never need to know. Think how proud she is going to be when we announce the good news to the assembly."

Gordon drank from his glass and gazed steadily at Harry as the three of them sat in silence. Harry knew he couldn't do anything but go along with the Vicar and the Squire, he had waited so long for Joan to say yes to his proposals of marriage and she was the love of his life. "When?" was the only word he could get out.

"Tomorrow." Gordon and Sam said together.

Harry sighed, "I need a drink."

"Allow me!" Reverend Weech raised his arm, "Joan, a pint for our new Engine Driver" Joan gave a squeal, threw the tea towel she was drying glasses with up in the air, ran from behind the counter and threw her arms around Harry. A broad grin spread across Harry's face and the worries of the last few days melted away.

They moved back into the main bar where Mr Valentine once again bought drinks for the company, slapping Harry on the back with exclamations of "I say!" and "Splendid!"

They celebrated on late into the night, Fred the landlord forgetting to call time, before they all parted company. During the celebrations they had found a trainee guard in Ron, the son of a local shop keeper, while his girlfriend Sally would help out at the station.

Dan assured everyone he would be fine in his own coach and set out back to the station. He groped his way along the track and finding the well wagon in the darkness he climbed up, dragged open the coach door and collapsed on to the sofa. Falling out of consciousness within seconds, his snoring was soon rattling the windows and echoing along the platform as he fell into a deep sleep.

CHAPTER 2

Thursday

—

New start

Knowing he could not rely on Dan to fire up *Thunderbolt*, The Reverend Weech came down to the station early on the next morning, nursing a slight headache as a result of the previous night's celebrations. Standing on the platform he heard Gordon arriving in the yard in the Bullnose Morris. "Good Morning Gordon, good morning Joan." the Vicar walked round into the yard as Gordon was helping Joan with some bottles.

"Good Morning Mr Weech, said Joan, we just passed Harry on the road – he says he will park his roller in the yard."

Gordon and Sam looked at each other – "Not for the first time" muttered Gordon.

"Is that Seth?" The Vicar shielded his eyes with his right hand as he looked up the line towards the shed. "He said he had rescued the bar counter and some seats from the wrecked coach, he must have come down early to fit them."

Joan put some of the bottles down onto the ground as Seth opened the crossing gates, his tool bag over his shoulder, walking towards them. He screwed his nose up, "There is some smell in that coach Reverend, that Dan has got it smelling to high heaven!"

"Oh no!" said Joan. Leaving her bottles on the ground she hurried towards the shed, followed by Gordon and Sam. Joan opened the door, and was hit by the combination of a powerful smell and the deafening sound of Dan's snoring.

"Oh, my goodness, what a mess!" Joan put a hand to her nose, Dan was lying half dressed face down on the sofa face, his boots were off and there was more foot visible than socks, which accounted for most of the smell.

His other clothes were scattered around the old carriage in every direction.

Seth put his head in the doorway, after first taking a deep breath of fresh air. "I don't know how I stood that while I was fixing that bar, you are going to have to do something about him, or will you be clearing up this mess every morning?"

"Get him outside Vicar while I try and fix this place up" Joan started picking up clothes and flinging them out of the coach, whilst Gordon and Sam picked Dan up and pulled him outside. Down by the track was an old Galvanized tank full of water, they dumped him into it, and he came up squealing like a whole sty of porkers. If the water had been colder he would have gone into shock, as it was he found his feet and bellowed at his tormentors.

"It is your own fault Dan, now get out of there and we will sort you out!" The Vicar was losing his patience.

"My best things have gone, I have no home – and now I have no clothes!" exclaimed Dan, trying to shake the worst of the water off whilst trying not to worsen his thundering headache.

"Look Dan, we will get you more clothes and you will have a home tonight." The Vicar offered his hand and helped Dan out of the galvanized tank.

Whilst this was going on Harry Hawkins had parked his roller and was coming along the line. "Harry," called the Vicar, "can you use the fire from the roller to fire up *Thunderbolt*? There is a strong bucket to carry it in on the footplate."

"Yes I suppose so, I have never stoked a railway engine before."

"It is the same as your roller, she already has water in, so you just need to make sure that you spread the fire evenly in the bed of the firebox – hopefully we will have Dan sorted out soon." Harry nodded, picked up the bucket and headed back towards his roller.

Gordon helped Joan and Seth to sort out the coach using plenty of disinfectant to get rid of the smell while the Vicar took the dripping and complaining Dan back to the station, where he used the telephone in the Stationmaster's office to call Mr Valentine.

Dan was drying himself in the booking office when the Vicar came back from telephoning. "That is you fixed up Dan, Mr Valentine is bringing some clothes down for you."

"I don't want cast-offs," moaned Dan, "my stuff was new."

"Your stuff was new at the end of the Great War Dan; it would take you a year to earn the price of one suit belonging to Mr Valentine, and a good year at that. Plus there's a good chance that the clothes will only be a year or two old anyway."

"Oh alright then." Dan allowed a small smile to creep on to his weather beaten face.

Mr Valentine arrived, chauffeured by his wife. He took two large Harrods boxes from the back seat and closed the car door with his right leg. "Good Morning Padre, good morning Dan, my wife sends her regards and here you are Dan – with my compliments." Dan looked at the boxes; he could hardly contain his excitement. *Thunderbolt* gave a toot, she was getting up steam.

"I must get on Mr Valentine, if you could see to Dan I will get back to *Thunderbolt* – oh and by the way we have a surprise for you!" So saying, the Vicar set off back along the track to the locomotive shed.

"I think she is about ready, Mr Weech, pressure seems to be up." Harry stepped back to let the Vicar see the gauge, *Thunderbolt* trembled, the footplate rattling the coal lying on the iron floor.

"You are right Harry she is ready, stand by." He looked back to see if Gordon was ready.

"Here we go, here we go again!" He moved the Regulator and *Thunderbolt* eased forwards towards the station and the waiting passengers. Mr Blakeworth followed by the early travellers had arrived and Emily had sorted out their ticket requirements, she had arrived shortly after Mr Valentine. Dan was changing in the Station Master's Office and his whoops of joy were causing Emily concern.

As *Thunderbolt* and its train drew to a stand alongside the booking office, Dan burst out through the door dressed as a carbon copy of Mr Valentine. "Hey Hey – Look at me, posh aren't I? Cor I'm too posh to fire that engine!"

Reverend Weech looked sternly at Dan. "If you do not get on this engine, you will suddenly find yourself without any clothes at all as I will personally put all of them in this firebox."

Dan had second thoughts, "I will put my old best ones on – won't be a tick!" he ducked back into the office and a few moments later reappeared in his wet clothes, jumping onto the footplate. "Let's go. I will dry off next to the fire." Steam was already rising from him.

Mr Valentine entered the coach, firstly met by a whiff of disinfectant, but facing him was a bar, his own rescued counter placed neatly against the back wall with Joan standing behind it. "Oh I say, I have died and gone to heaven!

Seth, you have created a miracle – I never thought I would see this sight again!" he looked around after he had settled himself against the counter. "And look at the seats! Oh congratulations once again my dear fellow."

Gordon blew his whistle and after Seth stepped back onto the platform, *Thunderbolt* started her first run of the day, the white smoke from her tall chimney drifting skywards. Mr Blakeworth settled down on one of the reclaimed seats and Mr Valentine started his first gin of the day. It was a bright sunny morning, there was no need for oilskins on the footplate this day. Reverend Weech showed Harry the controls and Dan demonstrated his firing skills.

"Why can't we use those water troughs just after we get on to the main line?" Asked Dan, leaning on his shovel. "It would save time at the water tower. Seth did a good job fixing it last week, but we waste time there – that's all I'm saying."

"We can't." said Reverend Weech.

"Why not?" Dan looked determined.

"For a start they're not ours and even if they were we haven't got a scoop on this locomotive, I can't remember when they first started using troughs."

"Who says it's not our water, who's going to know?"

"Somebody always knows. Don't ask me how, but somebody always does."

"What if I could get a scoop, what then?" Dan gave one of his knowing smiles.

"All right Dan if you find one I'll buy it, but how will we use it?" Reverend Weech resigned himself to the idea.

"Right, first there's this gap, here between the engine and tender – there's room for a pipe to go down there, then we gets a length of hose to go to the filler cap."

"All right so far Dan." Reverend Weech indicated to the fire hole door for Dan to feed the fire again, Dan grunted and threw four shovels full into the fire again.

"Now Reverend, I fix a bar to the end of the hose, and then when we come to those troughs I push the end into the water and it goes up the tube and into the tender tank – Bob's your uncle."

"How do you control the flow?"

Dan gave him his "I don't believe you" look.

"When we have enough water I lifts it clear, see, done!"

"Well," said the Reverend, "I suppose it might work – taking on water whilst moving could save us time."

"That's the way Reverend, that's the way – you know it makes sense."

Back at Titfield after the first run of the day, Dan went off to look for Seth while the Reverend checked over *Thunderbolt* and its train before retiring to the booking office and the comfort of its fire.

Returning to the locomotive's footplate for the second run, he saw an unfamiliar coil of tube laying on top of the tender.

"That looks like a piece of brake hose Dan, where did you get it?"

"Not saying it is, not saying it isn't, and I'm not saying where it comes from either. What I am saying is, it will work and this is how. Firstly this piece of steel rod connects to the hose end, with a funnel, right?"

"Right." everyone said together.

"Right, when we are coming up to the water troughs I puts the other end into the filler for the tank, this end with the funnel I pushes down this gap between the engine and tender and when we have enough I pulls it up."

Silence.

"Might work," said Gordon.

"It will." smiled Dan, pulling the scoop end back up.

Reverend Weech walked back with Gordon towards the guard's van. "Sam, does he know what happens when a tender gets too much water?" asked Gordon.

"I don't think so." replied the Reverend.

"Someone is bound to find out we are using their water." Gordon stepped onto the guards van.

"They usually do," said the Reverend as he turned and walked back towards the engine, waving to Mr Valentine and Joan as he went by.

They were approaching the main line and the water troughs. The Reverend had calculated that the water they had in the tank should get them to Mallingford and back to Titfield station if Dan's idea did not work.

"OK, you set Reverend? Hose is in the tank already and I'm ready to drop the scoop down." Dan lowered the end of the hose down between the engine and tender, the Reverend Weech looked at the troughs ahead. "Now!"

Dan pushed the hose end down into the water. The drag force caused by the hose entering the water at speed took Dan by surprise, he squawked and the thin round metal bar bucked and twisted in his hands. For a few seconds the water gushed up the hose and into the tender, filling it, then the force of water pressure lifted the hose out of the filler cap and into the air causing, a fountain of water into the slipstream sending it back towards Dan's coach.

Mr Valentine at this precise moment chose to push his head out of the window and was duly soaked; he pulled his head back into the coach. "Quite refreshing, Joan, I'll have another Gordon's I think."

Dan let go of the rod, which fell onto the track, the hose following it and spraying what water was left in it across the footplate and onto the crew. Dan was yelling. "Stop it! Stop it!" to nobody in particular, while the hose disappeared from sight and was cut to pieces by the train wheels.

"Well Dan," said Reverend Weech drying his face with his hand cloth, "I won't say I told you so."

"What do you mean?" said Dan. "All we need now is something fixed to the engine, and then the hose won't dance about."

"No Dan, nothing is to be fixed to the engine, sorry but that's the way it is."

"Well that's the last time you get any of my ideas. Oh, and by the way, you owe Seth a drink, said you would stand him one for fixing that rod to the end of the brake hose."

"So, it was a brake hose Dan, you know you should not have stolen it". Reverend Weech was tut tutting.

"I never did, I just found it, was an old piece, and there's no more".

"Good. Look never mind Dan, it was a good idea and it's just a shame it didn't work – that's all."

On they went, Reverend Weech with a song in his heart, Harry wondering if he had done the right thing and Dan gently steaming, giving off a smell of old moth balls and wet sink cloths. He was dry before they reached Mallingford.

Taff Jenkins did not much like trains, in fact his favourite saying was that they spoilt a signalman's job; but footplate crews he disliked intensely, they were a pushy, know-it-all lot, with not a brain between them. They only knew where they were going because of the rails, and who controls the rails – the signalman!

Taff was senior signalman in the Mallingford signal box, and had been there since the year dot. His tubby build, round face and small round black-framed spectacles made him a distinctive figure amongst the male staff. Taff always wore his railway cap, and no one really knew if he had any hair under it. Having let *Thunderbolt* and its train pass his first signal at clear he suddenly and without warning threw the next signal in front of *Thunderbolt* and its train back to danger.

"Here they come!" he shouted to his mate Ernie. "The Titfield Terrors, the Branch Line Buccaneers – how many years did it take us to Nationalise this ruddy railway, and then these buggers buy a little bit back – it wouldn't happen in Welsh Wales boyo."

The Reverend Weech closed the regulator, whistled for the guards brakes, put the engine into reverse and screwed the tender brake on.

Thunderbolt shuddered to a halt at the signal outside the box, with Dan grimly hanging on to the tender side to keep his footing.

"Steady on Reverend, that was a bit sharp."

Taff slid the window open and looked down on to *Thunderbolt*.

"You nearly went through that signal, when are you going to stop messing about on that pile of junk, and get yourselves a proper engine? Better still, get off my rails altogether!"

Dan turned his head round so quickly, he nearly lost his pipe.

"Pile of junk? Your rails? – Who do you think you are? And just what were you playing at putting the signal back like that, against all the regulations? Go back to chasing sheep if they will have you, you should be ashamed of yourself look you, call yourself a Welshman? And you can't sing for toffee!" Dan fired back, adding: "You could only get a job watching real men work – signal lackey!"

"So that's the *Thunderbolt* is it?" retorted Taff. "Seen this Ernie – a Rickety Vicar and a Desperate Dan, I don't know what to call Harry?"

"Who's desperate?" Dan snapped back.

"You must be to be on that footplate! You seen this Ernie – three nuts on a Bolt." Taff roared with laughter at his own joke. Ernie turned his back and put his hand to his mouth to keep his laughter in. "Get that heap of junk moving – I am clearing this signal right now!" Taff slammed the window shut, and the signal dropped.

"Righto Reverend, we have the road."

The Reverend Weech grasped the handle on the tender side and tried to turn it to release the brake. "It won't move Dan."

"Here, move out of the way – let me have a go." Dan grasped the handle and he too tried to turn it. "It won't move alright, the ratchet is stuck – it must be."

The signal box window slid open again. "Get a move on, traffic is building

up – shift that scrap iron of yours!" Taff shouted down to them.

"Can't!" said the Reverend, "The brake is stuck on."

"What?" shouted Taff "I just don't bloody believe it – move it or else!"

"Taff!" Ernie called, "I got Bert on the down local on the blower, asking why he's held at our home signal?"

"You can tell them the Titfield Teapot has got its wheels stuck." Ernie talked into the phone, and was nodding his head as he listened.

"Well?" asked Taff. "What?"

"They say shift it because the "Flyer" is running hard on their heels and control will be after their hides if they hold it up."

"Did you hear that?" Taff shouted out of the window.

"What?" replied Reverend Weech, straining to unwind the brake handle.

"If you don't move, The "Flyer is going to push you out of the way!" He thought for a moment. "Ernie, get the yard foreman on the blower."

"You should have oiled this brake gear, vicar." Dan gave The Reverend Weech a stern look.

"I say Dan – do I look like a driver who would skimp on his oiling up?" The Reverend was most put out.

"All I am saying is how this brake is stuck and it's not my fault, that's all I am saying." Dan scowled.

"Right, just shift that heap of junk now, I am going to get a shunter to come to move you out of the way!" Taff shouted out of the window.

"You can't do that, firstly these buffers are very old they might not take the impact, and we could damage the brakes, you must give us some time to sort this out." called back the Reverend Weech.

"Are you out of your tiny mind? You will have half the region blocked – get that heap of junk moving!" Taff's face was turning red.

"Call yourself a Welshman?" Dan bellowed back. "You should be ashamed – ashamed to side against those of us fighting for the little people."

"What? You calling yourselves little people then, what are you then boyo – Pixies?" Taff leaned into his box and grinned nastily at Ernie, the phone rang again and this time Taff picked it up. "Right, right, – I told them – right, right, right away." He scurried back to the window.

"You're for it, I wouldn't like to be in your shoes now – that was the big man on the phone. He says if you don't shift that thing of yours, he is going to phone London and have you all banned from these tracks." Taff now had a smile on his face, which rarely appeared whilst he was at work, and in the distance engine whistles were beginning to blow. Dan glowered back up at Taff.

"Watch out Reverend!" Harry had been standing to one side whilst all this activity had been going on, weighing up the situation. "This might work." Harry had removed a fire iron from the tool locker, and placed it behind the brake handle, tucking the end under the flat arm of the turning mechanism.

"Harry…." Reverend Weech gave a half warning.

Harry heaved, there was a twang from somewhere underneath the tender, and the brakes were released. "Quick, Reverend, take her away – *Thunderbolt* is free!" Harry put the iron away.

The Reverend Weech opened the regulator and they moved off and away towards their platform, Taff watching them from his signal box window.

"She seems all right Reverend." smiled Dan, patting Harry on the back.

"I hope so Dan." he replied, gingerly applying the brake to bring them to a stand after shutting off the regulator.

"We must have a good look at her when we get back to Titfield." said Reverend Weech with a sigh.

With shunting completed, fresh passengers on board and their signal cleared, Gordon blew his whistle and they moved out. Approaching Taff's box Dan held up two fingers towards Taff, who he could see glowering at them from his still open window.

"Dan." said The Reverend disapprovingly.

"Only Churchill's salute Reverend, only Churchill's salute – what is good enough for our Wartime Prime Minister is good enough for me. You know what, that Taff is the only Welshman I know that can't sing!" Reverend Weech gave a toot from the locomotive's whistle and they headed back towards their valley and Titfield. Taff slammed his window shut.

The run back to Titfield was happily without mishap, while inside Dan's coach business was brisk. Word was getting round to train enthusiasts and on each trip passenger numbers seemed to increase, it was so full on the run back that Mr Blakeworth had to stand at the bar accepting drinks from Mr Valentine.

On arrival at Titfield, Mr Blakeworth quickly went to have a word with Gordon. "I think we should have a meeting, I have picked up some information which we must discuss. I will be going to the Vicarage at seven, is that time all right for you? I will tell Sam so see you then too". What now, thought Gordon, as he let the brake off the van ready for running round and shunting the stock.

"Well done Harry, very well done!" Reverend Weech followed Harry down the track away from the shed.

Dan held back to have a word with Gordon. "That Harry was our enemy just days ago, I don't trust him." he glowered at Harry's back.

"Well he did lend us his steering chain on the inspection day, and whether we like it or not we do need more help" replied Gordon

"I can manage just fine – I'm fit I am." Dan's voice got just a little higher.

"That is not what you said yesterday – I'll probably see you in the Grasshopper later then."

Dan brightened. "That you will, I will be there in my new finery – I will be a proper gentleman. But you know what though; a gentleman should have a home!"

"You are right Dan; we will try and sort something out tonight."

The mantle clock struck seven in the rectory study as Emily announced the arrival of Gordon and Mr Blakeworth. "Come in! Come in gentlemen." Emily closed the door. "Sit down, sit down. My, after that business with Taff we had a grand day".

Reverend Weech sat down on the sofa. "That's the trouble Sam; it is going to get as busy as it was before we lost the old train – possibly even more. The old girl is struggling, you know she is."

Gordon looked across at Sam. "True enough, she is lacking a bit of power, but she will keep on going – she won't let us down." Sam looked at Mr Blakeworth who sat stern faced.

"Mr Weech you were desperate when we got her out of the museum, she was meant for just one run and she has already been going for nearly a week." Mr Blakeworth turned to the Squire "You know you have an obligation to provide a regular service between Titfield and Mallingford, the fact is you have got to get more suitable rolling stock."

Gordon and Sam, looked at each other, they knew that he was right.

Gordon turned to the Reverend Weech: "Sam, I have to tell you that someone is trying to cause us trouble, a certain person has asked the Mayor when *Thunderbolt* will return to the museum and who will pay if she has been damaged in any way" He continued, "I have written to the insurance company and stressed the urgency of our situation. It breaks my heart every time we pass 1401, and I am hoping we can get her moved for repair soon"

Sam sighed: "We must try and find another engine. There must be a spare engine somewhere, but we can't just go out and buy one – we just do not have the money".

Mr Blakeworth cut in. "I know one thing, Pearce and Crump have friends and they will be watching your every move, you may have a license, but you could lose it if someone complains that you are not offering a proper service."

He had said the words they did not want to hear and they knew he was right, Gordon looked dejected.

"Well we will have to hope for the best and try to come up with a solution, but for now we have a more pressing problem – what to do with Dan?"

"Dan?" Reverend Weech raised his right eyebrow.

"Yes" replied Gordon "Dan, we took his home and after this morning's performance he can't live there any more, we have to find him some accommodation." The room fell silent, but for the ticking of the mantle clock.

"Yes Gordon, but where?" Reverend Weech pondered.

"Don't look at me" said Mr Blakeworth. "My wife has a very considerate nature and is kindness itself, but Dan staying with us – never I'm afraid."

"I very much doubt if Dan would consider lodging with you anyway Mr Blakeworth, I think he would find it too confining." Reverend Weech shook his head.

"I know one place he would stay," Gordon cut in "the Grasshopper."

"By Jove Gordon, what a solution, what a solution" Reverend Weech chuckled, "well done."

Mr Blakeworth also rose to his feet. "But what about Fred?"

"Oh we will talk Fred round, a few pounds should sort everything out." replied Reverend Weech.

"I hope you are right Vicar, I think we should get moving don't you?" With that comment from Mr Blakeworth they all headed up the steps and out of the room.

The bar of the "Grasshopper" was crowded and the gathered company greeted the Vicar and the Squire as they entered, Mr Blakeworth having left them to return home. There before them standing at the bar were two visions of Mr Valentine, both wearing waistcoats of bright yellow plaid. The shorter and scruffier of the pair looked and beamed at them as they came in – Dan was very pleased with his new get up. Mr Valentine proper addressed the company: "Welcome Gentlemen, welcome, I am just about to buy wine for the company, please join us. Dan, Harry and I are drinking to a successful day." At the mention of Harry's name, Joan looked up and smiled.

They had their drinks and Gordon went to the bar to get another round. Fred served him and as Gordon received his change, he took the opportunity to have a word. "Fred do you still have the spare room free?"

"I have that, Mr Chesterford. Why, are you running out of space at the hall?

"Not exactly Fred, but I could get you a lodger." Gordon said, testing the ground.

'Well I am not saying I could not do with the extra cash." Fred was rubbing his chin with his right hand.

"Splendid, Dan can move in tonight then!"

"Dan!" Fred was not so sure. "Dan, why Dan? He has his own home!"

"Look Fred, it's a long story, but Dan needs a place and you have got one, so what do you say?"

"Oh all right Squire, but he had better behave himself." Fred was having second thoughts already.

"Dan, Dan, we have got you a place to stay."

Dan looked at Gordon with his sideways glance. "Where?"

"Here" said Gordon spreading his arms, Dan whooped with glee "Set 'em up Miss Hampton – I am your new lodger!"

Joan looked aghast at her father, nearly dropping the pint glass she was drying. "Dad if that old goat is staying here, you had better keep him under lock and key. I don't want to see him wandering about in his shirt tails."

"It will be fine Joan I am sure." Fred crossed his fingers.

At the final, "Time Gentlemen Please." Fred got the last customer out of the door.

"I will have another one Fred." Dan was sitting at a table with his legs resting on a chair and a nearly full pint in his hand.

"No you will not." replied Fred, weary from a long day.

"Yes I can." said Dan "I am a resident, I am, so I will have another pint."

"If I have any more lip Dan, you will be a resident out in the street and what would that do to your grand finery?" Dan mumbled under his breath, his perfect lodgings were not turning out quite as he expected. "Now" said the Landlord "I have got a few jobs to do, so get that pint down and I will take you up to your room." Ten minutes later and Dan followed Fred up the creaking stairs; opening the first door on the landing they entered a very pleasant room. "The bath room is down the passage so don't make a mess".

Dan looked about the room and at the lovely clean bed, with its big squashy pillows, and warm quilt. "Cor Lumme turned out nice again." Moving around the warm room, Dan touched each of the objects in it, the bed, the small round table; it also had a wash stand, and an oak wardrobe. "Cor, Very Posh", he chuckled; he sat on the bed and bounced up and down testing the comfort, "Great."

His gaze moved around the warm yellow lit room, his mouth was dry – a drink was what he needed. "I'm a resident I am," he muttered "So Fred if you don't want to get me a drink, I will get one myself." Once he thought he'd heard Fred go to bed, he tip toed to the door, lifted the latch and peered out into the gloom, no lights anywhere. "He He."

Dan moved silently towards the stairs, and shushing them as the treads creaked as they took his weight, he was soon standing in the empty bar, lit now by the bright moonlight.

"Right Dan and what would you like? I will have a pint and put it on my bill, Squire will pay." He chuckled as he removed the tea towel from the pump handles, Dan could pull a pint; he had watched the operation man and boy for the last forty years and with foaming pint, he sat at a table and knocked it back. "Another? I don't mind if I do!" he repeated the operation several times, and with the beer he had drank during the evening, he was now drunk.

Company was what he wanted; Dan always preferred to drink in company so he focused his eyes on the front door and staggered towards it. After fumbling with the bolts he flung it wide open with a loud bang, staggering out into the night, he flung his head back and shouted at the moon. "Who wants a drink, come on now, come and have a drink with Dan!" Shouting with his head back had upset his balance and he staggered back a few steps. The village was quiet, not a sound. Fred and Joan's rooms were at the back of the pub and so they heard nothing. "That's it nobody wants to know, well I will drink alone." Staggering back into the pub to pull another pint, Dan's legs finely gave out on him and he slowly slid down to the floor and passed out.

CHAPTER 3

Friday

—

New tactics

Gordon received an early phone call from a very upset Fred. "Squire, it's Dan, he came down during the night and helped himself to my beer. The old so and so unlocked the door and it must have been open all night – it's not on Squire, it's just not on."

"Oh, I am so sorry Fred. Look we will take care of any expense – where is he now?"

"The last time I looked he was lying on my bar floor".

"Throw a bucket of water over him and get him sober Fred, we need the old fool."

Gordon was looking round for his trousers.

"Right Squire I will wake the old soak up, see you later." Fred put the phone down and looked from his little office through to the bar, a tight lipped smile and an avenging look crossed his face as he went and filled a bucket. Every last drop of water splashed across Dan's sleeping body; the icy cold water shocked him awake.

"Agh – Get off me!" for the second day in a row Dan woke up wet.

"If you don't get sorted out right now, you are going to get another one of those and keep away from my beer pumps you old drunk!" Dan's head was throbbing; he looked up at Fred with pleading eyes. "Ooohh…"

"Serves you right." Fred turned towards the tap again.

"Alright, I'm getting up!" said Dan.

"You had better, Joan is down soon to get breakfast and the Squire says he is coming to get you, so hurry up."

Dan sat down at the table with a squelch. "Look at my new things." he complained to Joan as she put his eggs and bacon in front of him.

"Get that down you and put your other stuff on and I will dry them for you." Joan looked out of the kitchen window as Harry pulled up on his old motor bike. "Look, here's my Harry now."

Dan pushed the food into his mouth "I can tell you about your Harry…" he started to say.

"What are you on about?" Joan turned from the window, Harry called out to Joan.

"Nothing." said Dan, the rest of his message now under his breath – he did not trust Harry. The breakfast over, both Harry and Dan stood in front of the pub waiting. The Squire drew up in the Bullnosed Morris with the trailer at the back.

"You coming with us Harry?" Gordon swung the door open for Dan.

"I will use my bike Squire, I will get to the shed and start firing her up."

Gordon and Dan pulled away heading for the station, the trailer bouncing along after them.

Today they pulled alongside the platform on time, and waiting was Mr Blakeworth with an envelope in his hand. "Gordon look at this, it's from Pearce and Crump, they want me to visit them – something about our mutual advantage."

Gordon handed back the letter and envelope." Can you go and see them?"

"Yes, as a lawyer I can go at any time, they are on remand so they can have visitors every day, my visit would be what you would call a special one, besides I know the Governor quite well."

The day being sunny and warm, they had railway enthusiasts as well as their local passengers, so Dan's carriage was quite crowded. As the Vicar eased *Thunderbolt* forward he looked round at Dan and Harry. "I think we are going to have to reduce the passenger numbers, poor Mr Valentine has hardly any space at the bar!"

Thunderbolt headed off on her first journey towards Mallingford and the day was underway.

Seth and young Ron were walking down the track heading for the water tower, carrying tools "What are we going to do today Seth?" young Ron asked.

"I just did a sort of temporary job filling those holes in the water tower, now we are going to melt some pitch and cover the patches, seeing as there is still a little bit of water coming out."

"We should have used one of those trolley things, this stuff is heavy."

Young Ron was not happy.

"Look, on a lovely day like today a little walk will do you no harm. Did you know that this was not the first time that the *Thunderbolt* had been taken out of the museum?"

"Go on" said Ron.

"Look here is the tower; I hope you have noticed there are no pots and pans lying about the place. After that carry on when someone put holes in it, it was me that had to tidy up. I had to take all the stuff they had borrowed from Beales farm back again, it took me a while I can tell you, and what did I get – just a *Oh, well done Seth.* It takes more than just riding on a footplate to run a railway you know. I hope they drained the tank like I asked them to. We will put this pitch inside to seal the holes up properly, but first we have to melt it, so let's get a fire started, and I will tell you the story." They fixed up a fire underneath the pitch pot, to melt it, and then Seth and Ron found a comfortable spot near to the Tower to wait.

"It was in April of 1942, me, Dan, Mr Valentine, and the Vicar were all in the Home Guard, do you know what they called it before they changed the name, the LDV, it stood for the Local Defense Volunteers, otherwise known as Look, Duck, and Vanish."

"Go on!" Ron was now giving Seth his full attention.

"Yes, it was a moonlit night, one we used to call a Bombers moon, bright as daylight and it was then we heard them. German bombers that were heading for Bath, and Mallingford stood in the way. It was what they called a Baedeker raid, they were out really to just destroy old buildings, and they were using what they called Chandelier flares, Incendiaries, and High Explosives, but they were also after the *Thunderbolt*."

"Why the *Thunderbolt*?" Ron could hardly believe what he was hearing.

"Because, they knew that *Thunderbolt* was in the museum and they also knew she was the oldest working steam engine in the country, they wanted her gone."

"What happened?"

"It was the Vicar, he just knew he had to get *Thunderbolt* out, so we all went to Mallingford, and with the help of the local fire brigade, we manhandled her down the steps, and then we used a truck to get her to the station. Lucky we did, because just after that the Dorniers and Junkers bombers came over dropping their loads and there was fire and explosions all over the place."

"That fire is going well." Ron looked over towards the fire crackling away under the tower.

"It will be fine. Now there was a tank engine in steam at the station, which we hitched to *Thunderbolt*, and we set off for Titfield, going like the clappers. The bombs were starting to fall behind us, the ground was shaking, and dust was everywhere."

"Are you sure that fire is alright?" Ron was enjoying the story, but was a bit concerned about the fire.

"Never mind about the fire! We were travelling mind, both engines were rocking the speed they were going at, and the Vicar shouted, "There's a plane following us" and would you believe it, the darn thing started to machine gun us."

"Blooming heck!" Ron gasped, "Actual bullets?"

"What do you think he was firing at us, sweets? Of course they were bullets, anyway the Vicar said we would head for the tunnel, and all the time the bomber was firing, then turning round and coming back, it was touch and go, but we made it into a tunnel. Luckily there was not another train due, so we stayed where we were until the raid was over, then we took *Thunderbolt* back to Titfield and hid her, they came back the next night and pounded Bath again."

"Seth, look at the fire! The grass is alight – quick, what are we going to do?" Ron got to his feet.

Thunderbolt was returning from Mallingford and Dan saw the smoke coming from the water tower, he quickly reached under the coal, pulled back the tarpaulin and retrieved his shotgun. "Stand back Reverend, they are trying again, I will blow their heads off!" and with that Dan fired both barrels towards the water tower, Seth and Ron dived for cover. *Thunderbolt* eased to a stop right beside the water tower, the passengers looking out of Dan's windows.

"Steady Dan, its Seth and young Ron! What are you playing at Seth? I thought you were going to repair it, not burn it down! Kick the fire out, and turn the water on again, it will have to do, it won't lose too much water if we leave it for the moment." They waited whilst the fire was put out, then with two more on the footplate they headed back for Titfield.

Mr Blakeworth discovered he had the morning free, so he contacted the governor of Mallingford Prison and arranged a visit for eleven o'clock. An inner gate clanged behind them as Pearce and Crump, dressed in their hairy brown remand suits, stood in the doorway, no bravado now, they looked nervous and he could see they were glad to see him. The pleasantries over, they sat opposite Mr Blakeworth.

"Mr Blakeworth, you must know we meant no harm, we did not really mean to wreck the train, honestly, just cause a little damage, a little delay." Crump looked at Pearce.

"That is right Mr Blakeworth, no harm, no harm at all."

"Whatever you intended the train has been wrecked which has caused very great inconvenience, quite apart from the fact that I was put in great danger" Mr Blakeworth's face had turned quite red. "I have not come here to listen to your excuses, so state your business." Mr.Blakeworth was curt and to the point.

"Right Mr Blakeworth, cards on the table, Crump and I want to give our bus to the Railway as some recompense for the damage."

"Not that we are admitting anything" butted in Crump.

Mr Blakeworth fixed him with a beady stare, and then looked directly at Pearce. "What use is a bus to a Railway?"

"Well they could use it for collecting passengers from outlying hamlets, Crump and I thought of that just the other day." Pearce was trying.

"Don't you need to have a special driving license for a bus?"

"Well yes, they could hire a driver easy." Crump was trying to back up his partner.

"I have written to the garage, when the repairs are done they will deliver it to Titfield Station."

"I suppose it is an asset, but of course accepting it would not alter the course of any proceedings." Mr Blakeworth was making sure that Pearce and Crump did not get any wrong ideas.

"Of course if you were to put in a good word for us, it would help." Crump was just a little smarmy. "How is the engine running, is it keeping good time? And how is Harry Hawkins doing?"

Mr Blakeworth hesitated slightly before answering the last two questions. "The *Thunderbolt* is actually running very well, helped in fact by Harry Hawkins himself."

Pearce and Crump's jaws both dropped.

"Harry Hawkins working for the Railway and not on his roller?" Pearce's voice trailed away to nothing as he and Crump looked at each other in disbelief.

"Yes, in fact Mr Weech and the Squire are increasing the railway staff in readiness for more rolling stock and more frequent services." Mr Blakeworth hoped he was not jumping the gun, quite frankly he did not have any idea as to their future plans apart from what they discussed the other day. "Have you any other business you wish to discuss?" Mr.Blakeworth checked his pocket watch.

"I don't think so." replied Pearce "If we could get in touch with you again if we need to?"

"I am sure that would be in order, the Titfield Railway Company are my clients." Mr Blakeworth rose to his feet and picked up his brief case, the Prison Officer who had been quietly sitting at the back of the room told Pearce and Crump to remain seated.

By the time Mr Blakeworth was back in his office, Pearce and Crump had been returned to their cell.

"I don't believe it, how come they did not rumble Harry Hawkins?" Pearce sat on a cell chair next to their little table.

"What do you think Alec?" Crump sat on the lower bunk bed.

"What is his game? He must be thinking if he keeps his head down, and works for the other side….maybe they don't know about him, he could be our eyes and ears on the outside." Pearce was considering the options.

"We don't need him, we have still got friends on the outside" Crump was looking expectantly at his partner.

"Now listen, all they have got on us is you shooting your mouth off."

"I couldn't help it Alec, I panicked."

"Right now you change your story and then we………" The cell door banged open and they both jumped.

"Dinner!" said the Officer.

On the journey back to Titfield Mr Blakeworth stood at the bar with Mr.Valentine and Joan. "Pearce and Crump want to give us their bus."

"By Jove Mr Blakeworth, by Jove. It just keeps getting better, another drink Joan my dear." Mr Valentine patted her hand, Joan poured out two drinks, and Mr Blakeworth did not try to refuse.

"My Harry says the old girl is feeling her age, maybe we will need a bus before too long."

"Oh Nil desperandum, Joan my dear – I am sure it will not come to that." Mr Valentine swayed his glass with the motion of the train, so as not to spill a drop.

"We must speak to the Squire, and I wish we could do something about this infernal crush." said Mr Blakeworth, who was getting pushed up against the bar by the packed bodies of railway enthusiasts. They arrived at Titfield and Dan's coach emptied, Mr Blakeworth got out a little flustered.

Mr Valentine followed waved to his fellow passengers. "Goodbye, goodbye, and do come again!"

Mr Blakeworth glared at him. "Mr Valentine I do not want them to come back again, I want the passenger numbers to be as they used to be."

"But Mr Blakeworth." Mr Valentine looked shocked. "Paying customers – money!"

"But don't you understand, *Thunderbolt* will not be running much longer if they keep coming back, it is too much weight for her, she will break down."

Mr Valentine was silenced and stood looking at *Thunderbolt* quietly hissing, being attended to by Dan and Harry. The Squire and the Vicar were by now talking to Mr Blakeworth and hearing his news.

"But what would we do with a bus?" the Reverend asked.

"Well" said Mr Blakeworth, looking up at the surrounding hills "Pearce and Crump were talking about a collection service, going round the hamlets and delivering the people to the station."

"That is a thought" Said Gordon.

Seth strolled into the station yard just as they had locked up the building and were ready to go, Mr Blakeworth called Seth over. "Could we have a word Seth?'

"Certainly Mr Blakeworth Sir."

"Why don't you and Dan go on to the pub Harry, there is no need to keep you two waiting here."

Reverend Weech waved them off, and he and the others grouped around Seth. "We have a problem Seth, too many passengers, what could we do about it.?"

"Too many! Why a couple of weeks ago you couldn't get enough."

"True Seth, true, but we have too many railway enthusiasts and the old girl is starting to struggle with the load, we have to stop them coming, at least for a while."

"Ah" Seth.pondered "what if they couldn't find Titfield?"

"What have you got in mind?" the Reverend asked.

"We could do what we did at the start of the War."

"What was that?" Asked Gordon.

"Why we changed all the signposts round, nobody knew if they was coming or going and that was the ones who had lived round here all their lives." Seth broke off laughing heartily.

"I say Seth, well done, well done, but I don't think that is legal now." Reverend Weech looked around at his fellow conspirators. "They would think kids had done it that is all – when do you want it done?"

"Tomorrow!" Seth, Gordon and Mr Blakeworth all said together.

"Best if I starts about five miles out and works back in, most signs are those metal ones, a couple of spanners and a hammer should do it."

"You can borrow the car Seth," Gordon said enthusiastically.

"Don't you worry Gentlemen; Seth will do the job right."

"That is fine. Now all we have to worry about is Dan, I am sure that if he carries on the way he has been Fred will evict him."

Seth smiled and looked at Reverend Weech. "If I was you Vicar, I would put a shot of Vodka in Dan's last couple of pints. Makes him go all funny Vodka does, makes him go off sound to sleep!"

The Reverend's face relaxed. "Could I leave that up to you Gordon? I must get on with the sermon tonight."

"Of course Sam, I will mention it to Fred." Gordon went on to the Grasshopper whilst Reverend Weech and Mr Blakeworth headed for home. The Vodka worked a treat. Fred slipped a shot into Dan's second to last pint and a double into the last one and as Dan finished it off he did not even hear Fred call "Time Gentlemen Please" his eyes were already closing. After finishing off in the bar, Fred and Joan took an arm each and pulled Dan from his chair and up the stairs to his room.

CHAPTER 4

Saturday

—

Back to the war

The cocks were still crowing in the nearby fields heralding another hot sunny Saturday, when Dan was called from his bed. He came down to breakfast and ate heartily everything that Joan put in front of him.

"All right Dan?" Asked Fred coming in from the yard.

"I'm fine Fred, fine I am, not even a hangover." Fred looked over Dan's head and gave Joan a sly look and a wink.

Reverend Weech stood by *Thunderbolt* his oil can in his hand, with a look of astonishment as Dan walked up with a hearty song.

We come along on Saturday morning greeting everybody with a smile,
We come along on Saturday morning knowing it's well worth while,
As members of the ODEON club we all intend to be,
Good citizens when we grow up and champions of the free,
We come along on Saturday morning, greeting everybody with a smile,
Smile, smile, greeting everybody with a smile.

With a cheery "Mornin' Reverend" and still whistling, he swung himself aboard *Thunderbolt* to light her up.

"Well bless my soul, bless my soul." Reverend Weech shook his head in wonderment.

Gordon left the Morris in the yard for Seth and *Thunderbolt* set off on time with a few locals going shopping and a crowd of enthusiasts who were jostling a not very happy Mr Valentine up against his bar counter. Harry took his turn with the firing, and checking the gauges, but he was not happy. That morning by the early post he had received a letter from Mallingford Prison.

It was close to eleven o'clock when Seth climbed on top of the stone wall at a wide crossroad three miles from Titfield. Broad grass verges made this an ideal location for his plan and the sun was scorching down as Seth steadied himself against the signpost. A few turns of his ring spanner after he had cracked the built up layers of paint on the bolt heads, a quick tap with his two pound hammer, and the Titfield sign was pointing in the opposite direction to the town bearing its name.

Seth had just slid down, and was in the field behind the wall and leaning comfortably over it when the MG. sports car screeched to a halt, kicking up the dust from the roadside as it stopped beside him. "I say!" Said the driver, a young fellow wearing a County Cap, Harris Tweed jacket and fawn cords. His pretty young companion wore a flowery dress with a tiny headscarf partly covering her blonde hair. "I say there!"

Seth never answered anyone who addressed him with "I Say." and placing a wheat stalk in his mouth, he continued to stare implacably across the valley. The county cap with the young city gent underneath it got out of the MG. "I say old boy, which way is Titfield? We want to go and see that *Thunderbolt* thingy." His tone was not quite as haughty as it had been before. Seth waggled the wheat stalk with his mouth and slowly looked up at the sign; the young driver followed his gaze. "I am sure we have been down there already, we've been going round in bally circles, I'm sure we've been down there before."

"Titfield you says." Seth put on his country drawl, he thought about putting in some extra Aahhhs as well. "You'm having difficulty finding Titfield, why it has been round here for years it has."

"It might have been ruddy well round here for years, but I can't find it!"

Seth looked over towards the car, the young girl smiled and waved to him. "Don't that young lady know either?" Seth scratched his head and waggled his straw.

"No, she ruddy well does not." The young city gent was now getting quite cross.

"Uuuummmm well if I was going to Titfield, I wouldn't go from here." Seth fixed him with a stare.

"What?"

"No, I wouldn't go from here; I'd go from way back there." Seth pointed in the direction from which the car had come.

"What?" The young man's voice rose in exasperation.

"In fact if you can't find a little place like Titfield, I would look for something a bit bigger, 'twould be the best probably." Seth fixed him with a stare.

"Look!" the young man's temper was rising, "I only want to know the right road for Titfield. Please – that's all I want!"

"A hot young gentleman such as yourself would be better off going to Mallingford, and on the road to Mallingford is a grand pub, serves fine ale in there it does. You could treat the nice young lady to a cool drink and maybe a spot of lunch, she looks a fine young lady she does." Seth wiggled the straw whilst fixing the young man with a steady gaze, he could see little beads of sweat breaking out on his questioner's brow. The young man turned towards his car, and then turned back to Seth in exasperation.

"Mallingford – are you sure?"

"Best way, best way by far Mallingford is. As I says, too hot a day to keep that nice young lady out in the sun." the straw moved from left to right in Seth's mouth, the young man looked at Seth, his eyes questioning.

"Mallingford." It was said with a resigned sigh.

"Yep, straight on up there." Seth pointed. "Look for the Bell."

The young man returned to the car, said something to the girl which Seth could not hear, climbed in, crashed the door closed and roared off in the direction Seth had pointed out.

The Morris was parked at the field entrance; Seth chuckled to himself, as he reversed out on to the road. "He'll find the Bell, but he won't find Mallingford." He chugged slowly away from the cross roads, bounded on all sides by golden wheat fields, which he left to the hot sun and the calling crows.

Thunderbolt was back in her shed and Gordon, Reverend Weech, and Dan were walking away down the track towards the station, Harry sat on the edge of the water trough and opened his letter, he read it again. "Use your Roller as you did before, but this time everything must roll. You would not want anyone to know what we know – Sunday night, you will be watched." Harry knew Pearce and Crump would not let go, his stomach was churning, he wiped his brow – what was he going to do?

If they decided to say he was in it with them he would be behind bars before he knew it. In the last few days he had come to like working on the railway, he loved the attention he was getting from Joan and he felt part of things, but what was he going to do? If he did nothing Pearce and Crump would involve him, but if he wrecked the train then the Squire,

Reverend Weech and the rest would soon work things out, so he would go to prison anyway, in all events he would lose Joan. He folded the letter and put it into his trouser pocket, and started slowly walking back towards the station, his brain was racing, he stopped in his tracks, maybe, maybe, a plan was forming.

He did not want to wreck the train, but he did not want to lose Joan. Harry lived on the outskirts of Titfield; if he took a round-about-route he could reach the station without going though the village, or near the Squire's place. He did not want to do anything, but if he had to…

Emily had left William to run the station, she needed to catch up with her housekeeping duties. She surveyed the large sitting room which the Reverend also used as his office, running trains is all very well and good, but dust waits for no one, she thought bringing up her feather duster. If there was a bit of dust on that engine of his he would have his cloth out straightaway, but here, he would happily wade through it.

She started with the mantelpiece with its silver framed photographs, going on her tip toes to remove the first one. It showed a young couple's wedding day, the bride wearing the fashion of the day, the young groom in his captain's uniform, and dog collar – the Reverend had changed in the passing years.

Emily ran the duster round the embossed frame, flicked the mantelpiece and replaced it back in its original position. Moving to the next one, which contained a photo of a young boy smiling out at the camera, her hand trembled slightly as she held it, and she gently brushed the surface. He had been so young, so full of life, had a son ever been so loved, so idolized as him. He had nearly cost his Mother her life, and after his birth she was never the same. "Young Brian." Sighed Emily.

She remembered the day six years later that the Doctor had called, for Emily had come to look after the house after Brian's birth. The house was still, and then came that horrendous wail, which was tearing itself from his Mother's body, the sound echoing around the house. Cancer – It had taken a strong hold and within the week the little six year old was dead. Both Sam and Ruth were devastated; not only Titfield, but the whole valley mourned their loss. Through it all Sam had carried on, his parish was his life and his faith did not waiver. Sighing again she placed the frame carefully back on the mantelpiece.

Completing her dusting, she worked her way around the sunlit room to the Reverend's desk; again photo frames of Ruth and Brian, an identical set were sitting on his bedside table, so he could see them last thing at night and first thing in the morning. Emily was slight of frame, barely reaching five foot, but even to her Ruth, though a little taller, had appeared delicate. In the photograph she was wearing the outfit she wore when the Reverend had placed the wireless in the church that Sunday morning when the Prime Minister had told the nation that once again we were at war. It was as if Ruth had crumbled like a flower after that day.

She and Sam had nursed Ruth through the dark days of Dunkirk, and when in that glorious September, the few had beaten back the enemy, Ruth had passed away sitting in the garden. The Reverend had faced her death like the old soldier he had been, his faith, his great love of the railway and his increasing war work had kept him going.

Emily flicked the feather duster across the mahogany writing set, with its large silver ink pots at each end, using her yellow duster she polished the little brass plate set into the wood. Inscribed, *To our friend Mr Samuel Weech with our thanks, Felicity and Walter Valentine*. Emily smiled. It was odd, she thought, they are good friends but they had always used their surnames and never got too close and yet now they were as thick as thieves with the railway business. Emily looked round the room once again. "That will have to do for now, I must keep this room looking somewhat normal in case he invites the Squire and Mr Blakeworth back here again."

CHAPTER 5

Sunday

—

Short day

They ran a short day service that Sunday, Reverend Weech attending his Church and Congregation and Mr Valentine attending the Grasshopper; Harry, Dan, and Gordon running *Thunderbolt* in the afternoon. In spite of the road signposts being moved, they still ran to nearly full capacity – all railway enthusiasts.

Harry acted as normally as he could. Driving *Thunderbolt* in the afternoon he nearly forgot his worries, he even suggested that they top up *Thunderbolt* with water on their last run back to Titfield. He was in the Grasshopper as usual until closing time and managed a quick kiss and cuddle with Joan before setting off for his cottage. He had set the fire before he had left for the pub, so he only had to put a match to it to light up the Roller's fire. By twelve thirty the pressure was up, the fire bed glowed red and level. He eased the throttle and she rumbled forward. He moved along the dark quiet country lanes, away from the village, in a wide arc to reach the station from the far side of Titfield. The moon was out and there were no clouds, so he had good visibility, but he worried that he could be easily seen and heard. After nearly an hour he could see the outline of the makeshift engine shed at the station.

He opened the crossing gates and got the roller onto the ground, next to the run round track. Standing on the roller driving platform, he could see *Thunderbolt* and her train through the gloom, but even after the hours spent firing and traveling he still was not sure what he was going to do. Harry had tried to say something to Joan earlier that evening, but she was talking about plans for the wedding. In the stillness he found a bit of comfort in lighting a cigarette.

"Hawkins, what are you doing? Get on with it," a man's voices called from the darkness, coming from somewhere near the shed.

"You had better start and pull it, or we will set fire to it, where it stands," a new voice.

"Wait a minute, wait a minute," Harry knew he was outnumbered.

"You had your chance Hawkins."

"I come didn't I – I am going to do it!" Harry was trying to see where the voices were coming from.

"All right then how about this to help you see what you are doing."

Out of the gloom two blazing torches arced from the fields beside the shed, and set fire to the straw bales lying against the engine shed. The flames licked quickly at the dry straw, and in no time they were reaching for the guards van. "Hoy, Hoy," Harry shouted and he put the roller in reverse and rumbled backwards as quickly as he could towards *Thunderbolt*, getting to six feet away before jumping down and pulling his drag chain from the roller, coupling up to *Thunderbolt*.

He then realised he had to get to the guards van to release the brake. After stumbling along the side of the train, he could see the flames; they were reaching the van as he climbed aboard. The lock pin was pulled and he quickly turned the brake wheel, it may have only taken a minute, but already the van was filling with smoke. As he came out onto the rear landing another flaming torch hit the roof of the van.

Harry hit the track running; he only had minutes now to save the train, it seemed ages before he reached the roller, his boots slid on the metal surface of the roller footplate as he reached forward and opened the throttle. The roller lurched forwards, the drag chain snapped taught and shook with the tension; he was starting to move a dead weight of over seventy tons. The throttle was now wide open as the roller slowly moved forwards, the flames licking over the shed silhouetting *Thunderbolt* and her train.

A thought came to Harry's head; he would never hear the end of it if he let Dan's carriage burn. Clearing the shed the train started to pick up a little speed. Now Harry realised what he had started, he now had to stop the train – he needed to try and bring it to a halt at the platform. Just past the platform end the gradient starts to fall away, if he could not hold the train before then, he would have carried out the wishes of Pearce and Crump's friends.

Harry was staring disaster in the face, seventy tons against seventy horse

power. Closing the throttle to let the roller come to a halt, Harry quickly jumped to the ground, first he had to move the drag chain to the front of the roller, and then run to the front of *Thunderbolt*, to unhook the drag chain. He risked being knocked down by her whilst unhooking, but he accomplished this and jumped aside, then he waited, first as the tender went by, then the wagon carrying Dan's coach.

The chain lay coiled by the track, the guards van came by. Harry had only one chance – he had to hook the chain onto the coupling. He did it at the first attempt and sprinted for the roller as fast as he could go. He had to reach the roller and get it moving forward before the chain became taught, if he did not, then the seventy tons would snap the chain and *Thunderbolt* would be lost.

Leaping back onto the roller, Harry opened the throttle. The chain was just lifting off the ground and his movement was now nearly matching that of *Thunderbolt*, which would save the chain from snapping – but now he had to stop the train. It was the normal way to bring the roller to a halt; Harry had done it a thousand times before, but this time he really did not know what was going to happen.

He grasped the forward-reverse lever and pulled it backwards, the ratchet clicked, the roller started to judder and slide and the chain was staining at every link – it could snap at any moment. "Oh heck." Harry could see that *Thunderbolt* and her train had slowed right down, but she was still moving. There was a high pile of stones which was used as track ballast off to the right; Harry figured if he pushed the roller into it, the stones might give him some extra drag.

Carefully he eased the roller over, watching the angle of the chain; a wrong angle could flip a roller over and if that happened Harry could be crushed. Stones were brushed from the side of the pile as Harry's roller buried itself into the ballast – the train slowed again, but was still inching forward. Once again Harry was off and running for the brake van, while keeping one eye on the tensioned chain. Clambering up into the cabin, Harry turned the brake wheel as fast as he could, the brake blocks crunched against the van wheels, and Harry locked the wheel in position. Jumping from the van platform, he ran along the side of the train and up on to *Thunderbolt's* footplate, to put the tender handbrake on and at last everything stopped.

Harry's legs were shaking like a jelly and his heart thumping, his chest was heaving as he fought to get his breath back. Slowly he swung himself off *Thunderbolt* and made his way back up the line, checking by what little light came from the moon, to see if the train had sustained any damage. The drag chain was as taught as an iron bar and the rollers pistons were still hammering, he could ease it off now as the train was balanced.

Stalemate. Now what was he going to do – he needed help. The flames still lit the sky and Harry saw three dark figures running from the fire towards him, which was help he did not want, they could undo his rescue and send *Thunderbolt* off down the gradient to certain destruction. He had a hammer in his toolbox up on the roller; it looked like Harry had a fight on his hands. Slowing the piston, he collected the hammer and jumped down to the ground. The figures were getting closer and Harry stood legs apart, slowly dropping the head of the hammer into the palm of his left hand in readiness. From the direction of the village came the sound of a fire engines bell, and then strong headlights, the figures turned and ran off in the direction they had come from.

Gordon and the Reverend Weech were following the fire engine in the Morris, and swung into the station yard just behind it. "Harry, Harry, by all that's merciful, are you all right?"

"I am fine Vicar, but I don't know about the shed."

"What happened, Harry?" Gordon had a torch and was shining it from the train to the roller.

"You will not believe me when I tell you."

"Come on Harry, by the looks of things you have pulled off a miracle." Reverend Weech was shaking his head.

"Well I was out with the roller." Harry started to answer.

"On a Sunday night, Harry?

"Yes Vicar, on a Sunday night, the roller needed a run."

"Come on Harry, we did not hear you coming through the village, why not tell us what really happened, before someone else comes along?" Gordon was watching the firemen dousing the last of the flames.

Harry pulled the letter from his pocket, and handed it to Gordon, who held the torch on it while he and the Vicar read it together. "So what are you going to do Harry?" Reverend Weech handed back the letter.

"Look Mr Weech I am damned no matter what I do. They say if I don't wreck the train they will tell on me and then I will be banged up in jail – so I will lose Joan no matter what! You are right I set off to do what they asked, and then when I got here three of Pearce and Crump's friends set light to the shed – I had to pull her out then."

"But Harry, how did she end up where she is?" Reverend Weech could not quite comprehend.

"I can see what Harry means, Sam, I know from my Navy days, you might start a weight moving, but you have a devil of a job to stop it, and as you said Harry pulled off a miracle."

"Harry I'm not sure what really brought you here tonight, but you saved the day, if that fire had taken hold we would have lost everything, so well done."

The Leading fireman came down the line towards them. "You were lucky, only the grass on the side of the line got burnt, that Old Dutch barn got scorched a bit, and mind there is not much left of your coal heap, good job your train wasn't in it."

"We can thank Harry for that," Reverend Weech patted Harry on the shoulder. The Leading hand looked from the train to the roller, "Now what?"

"We have to get her back onto the level, and my roller by its self cannot do it," Harry shrugged his shoulders.

"Can we help?" Asked the leading hand.

"If you have got chains you can help me move her, by both hauling at the same time."

Harry waved his hammer in the direction of the station, and the leading hand gave a puzzled look, Harry hurriedly slipped the hammer into his trouser pocket.

"I will get the appliance turned round, the track should take it alright and we have some good strong chains"

"If you get on the van brake Squire and if Mr Weech takes *Thunderbolt's* brake off first, then when we are set, both their fire engine and I will pull at the same time, you Squire let the brake off on the van as we take up the strain."

Gordon nodded agreement. The fire engine crew hauled their chain and hooked onto the brake van, then eased forward until their chain was as tight as Harry's.

"You get well clear of those chains Mr Weech, if one of those snaps it will have you clean in two," Harry called from the roller, "If a chain does go Squire, get ready to put your brake back on again."

"Ready." Shouted Gordon.

"Ready." Shouted the leading hand revving up his engine.

"On three," shouted Harry, holding the roller, whilst getting its engine running. "One, Two, Three!" Harry put the drive in.

Both fire engine and roller moved at the same time, the fire engine's tyres scrabbled for grip on the wooden sleepers whilst Harry's roller sent up a shower of stones into the air as its driving wheels searched for grip. Harry looked across at his allies and then his new luck held, they got their grip at the same moment and *Thunderbolt's* train inched slowly back on to the level track.

It took a further ten minutes before the train was standing alongside the platform, Gordon, Reverend Weech and Harry waved the fire engine and its crew away. "I'm worried those three might come back." Said Harry "I don't know who they are but they might be watching us right now."

"I don't think so Harry, why don't you see to your roller while we wait and see?"

So Harry walked across to tend to his roller leaving the Squire and Reverend Weech to consider their next move. "You know Sam tonight could just be the start of more trouble and we don't even know who these people are."

"We really did not know the last time Gordon, and I am worried about Harry too."

"I think after tonight Sam, Harry can take care of himself."

Harry damped down the roller's fire after putting it away into the station yard.

"I just remembered something" said the Reverend "that fireman mentioned something about the coal heap burning."

Sam looked worried, quickly they went down the track to see the damage – the coal heap was now just a couple of shovels full amongst a lot of smoking ash. "They have done more damage than I thought they had, it is very fortuitous *Thunderbolt* has a full tender, we should just have enough coal for a couple of runs."

"That's all right Sam, we can just fill her up at Mallingford tomorrow." Gordon was wondering why Sam was so worried.

"Ah but I forgot to pay the bill – we will not get any more coal tomorrow. I will pay of course but they have a rule, you order the coal one day and get it the next."

"We can tell them what happened Sam, they are sure to waive the rule if we explain – surely?" Gordon looked hopefully at Sam.

"You forget Gordon not everyone likes us, they will not change the rule, at least not for us." Sam slowly shook his head.

"So now what?" asked Harry, who had rejoined them after putting the roller away. "We have got to do something, I am not giving in now, and we will have to get some coal from somewhere – how about the villagers?"

"Well we don't have to use steam coal all the time, and she will smoke a bit, but who has coal at this time of year?" Sam looked at them both.

"We know someone who will know – Seth." Harry kicked at the little pile in front of him.

"Right that's settled, we can tell Seth in the morning and hopefully he will get enough to keep us going, I am sure he will but whatever happens we have done all we can here." Gordon turned towards the station and reaching the station yard, they all climbed into the Morris.

"Maybe you should tell Joan, Harry, you know.....about before." Reverend Weech tentatively put forward his idea as Gordon started the Morris. "We will rally round and give you our support."

"No, I cannot Vicar, not yet. I know I should tell her, but not just yet."

"Just as you like Harry." Reverend Weech quietly sighed.

CHAPTER 6

Monday

—

Fifth columns

The Squire had to pass Seth's cottage on his way to the station, which stood in a loop made by the road so that you could see into both front and back gardens. Gordon could see Seth scattering corn for his chickens. "Seth" he called, stopping close to the stone wall surrounding the garden and standing to get a better view. "We have a big problem, we need coal. There was a bit of a fire last night and we lost the whole heap."

"Go on. I never heard anything. Anyway I thought you got your coal at Mallingford, Welsh coal – Dan told me."

"Look Seth it is a long story and I need to get on, but we need all the coal you can get your hands on, there will be no coal available to us until later tomorrow. Could you go round the village and ask for donations – we will compensate everyone. Oh, and Seth could you take it to the station? Thanks Seth, see you later."

Gordon dropped down into his seat, and was about to pull away, when he stood up again.

"I will leave the car and trailer for you to use in the station yard." He dropped back down again and headed for Titfield.

"No poaching today," Seth muttered to himself throwing the last of the corn at the chickens. He looked about his well kept garden and up the beautiful green valley made even more striking in the glorious morning light. "God's Country" he thought to himself.

Mr Ruddock swept round the exclusive London square on his ex-paratroop folding scooter. "Morning Todd." they both picked up the scooter and carried it into the Ministry of Transport building as usual. He walked up the stairs and entered his office. "Morning Mr Clegg."

"Morning – I have had a letter here from Titfield." He passed it across the desk to Ruddock.

"Titfield, hmm, I thought they were doing quite well." Ruddock sat down and as he read the tightly worded pages his frown grew deeper. "I say, do you think this is true?" he turned the final page, and looked at the bottom. "Signed too, this is serious."

"I should think it is, implying that the rolling stock they used on the trial day was temporary that they don't have any other stock, and no relief crew either!"

Mr Ruddock carefully stroked his chin. "You know I said at the time, they could be taking too much on."

"I hope you read that bit about their activities during that trial run – I mean can you believe it? If I had known I would not have granted them their license."

"Well what now? Are you going to revoke it – might not be wise." Mr Ruddock still had a soft spot for the Titfield amateurs.

"No, but in view of the obvious local concern I will write and tell them I will be inspecting their rolling stock and manning levels on Tuesday week."

"Quite right" said Mr Ruddock, voicing solidarity with his colleague. Not long after this conversation though Mr Clegg had to go to see the Minister. As soon as he had gone Mr Ruddock picked up the telephone. "Could you get me the town clerk at Mallingford…"

After collecting the Morris and its trailer from the station yard, Seth drove it to the Grasshopper. "You there Fred?" Seth looked in at the kitchen door.

"Hallo." Fred called from the cellar.

"You heard the latest, Fred? The Squire wants some coal."

Fred came into the kitchen looking a little flustered, "I heard last night."

"Have you got any? Mind you they usually has that Welsh coal."

"Look, I haven't heard mine say ruddy Yachi Da so it must be English – do you want it or not?"

"Course I do, how much you got?"

"Probably half a trailer full, but according to what they were saying last night you are going to need a lot more than that. You know where it is, leave me a little bit though O.K."

"Righto Fred, I'll collect yours then I might go and see the Kind twins."

"Good luck," said Fred and went back to his cellar.

Thunderbolt was approaching the Mallingford sidings, and Harry was scraping the shovel around the tender trying to gather the coal that was left. "There are only about six shovelfuls left, that's not enough to get back to Titfield – we have got to get some more coal." They were approaching three Hall class locos on a parallel siding simmering quietly in the warm sunshine. "Stop just there Reverend, I have an idea." Harry waved to the crew of the nearest Hall. "Hi mate, can you give us some coal, they will not give us any until tomorrow and we're nearly out – any chance of a few shovels full?"

The driver of the Hall leaned out of the cab, and looked down into *Thunderbolt*'s tender.

"Looks like you are running on fumes Mate – George, shoot some coal down to the old girl; I'll let the lads know up the line. Hurry up – the yard gaffer might be watching!" With that the driver swung down from the cab and headed towards the other locomotives, George heaved the coal out of his tender and across the gap, to reach *Thunderbolt* down below. The driver ran back towards them. "Quick, the yard boss is about – move her slowly forwards and the lads will shoot you another load as you go by."

"Good on you mate!" Harry waved to the driver. "On you go Reverend." *Thunderbolt* eased forward and as they passed slowly by the next two Halls their firemen shovelled coal into their tender.

"Thank you, thank you so much. We hope we can do the same for you some time – bless you all!" Reverend Weech smiled up at the crews as they passed by, dust rising from the newly acquired coal in their tender. He delicately opened the regulator to give *Thunderbolt* a little more momentum and they ran into the platform and drew to a halt, Reverend Weech looked at his watch. "Still on time!"

Gordon came up from the guard's van. "Well done you two, I got a little dusty as we passed the Halls and I wondered what you were up to at first, but just look at that coal! Let's hope Seth has the same kind of luck back at Titfield." Harry wiped the sweat from his neck with his handkerchief.

Seth could feel the warm sun on his back as he filled the trailer from Fred's coal bunker, he checked his pocket watch. "Might just be in time for a cuppa," he mused.

The Kind twins lived on the edge of the village, in a picture postcard cottage. Surrounded by a well kept and large garden the cottage stood well back from the road. They were in the front garden as Seth pulled up; he gave them a toot on the horn.

They were the wrong side of sixty, but they tried their best with powder and lipstick, applying both liberally. Both being nearly six feet tall, they looked rather elegant in light blue silk summer dresses.

"Morning Miss Patty, Morning Miss Primrose, what a lovely day!" Seth looked around admiring the flowers.

"Why Seth," they said in unison, "what brings you here – would you like a cup of tea?"

"Only if you have got nothing stronger." They did sometimes have a quite nice Cider, Seth was hopeful. "I'm after some coal for the Squire; they had a bit of trouble last night and lost all of theirs – have you got any to spare?"

"Why Seth, we had a delivery on Friday, of course you can take as much as you need anything we can do to help that nice Squire and Reverend Weech."

"That's very kind of you ladies; they need enough coal to keep the old engine going until tomorrow so I will have that cup of tea and load up." Seth sat down on one of the wrought iron chairs placed around the table and admired the roses.

Thunderbolt arrived back at Titfield Station at noon. Seth was waiting on the platform with the trailer filled with coal and Reverend Weech greeted him warmly. "I say, well done Seth – we will need all of that! Would you mind helping Dan and Harry load up as I must have a word with the Squire." So saying, he walked back towards the guards van, just behind the engine. "Gordon I don't believe it, but Mr Blakeworth assures me it is true – the Ministry are coming back to inspect us again and I know they will want to see our original rolling stock." He removed his cap and mopped his brow.

"Well the insurance company has released funds, so we can raise 1401 and the carriage. Tomorrow evening after the last run, two cranes will lift them up the embankment and take them away for repair." At least Gordon was trying to keep positive.

The Reverend smiled and pulled out his pocket watch to check the time. "Are you all loaded up Gordon? We'd better get started back to Mallingford"

Seth hitched the trailer back on to the Morris and set off to locate more coal supplies.

"At least we are running fairly light on this trip; the old girl wasn't sounding too happy on that last run back from Mallingford." After the run around, the three footplate crew climbed aboard *Thunderbolt* and Gordon stepped on to the guards van and blew his whistle.

In Dan's former home Joan handed Mr Valentine his first drink of the run and on the footplate Reverend Weech stood back and let Harry drive *Thunderbolt*. "He has been a godsend," he thought to himself, "what a pity he had been against the railway at the start". After they had passed the junction Harry took a spell at the firing while Dan drew on his pipe whilst keeping a wary eye on Harry – he still did not trust him.

Seth toiled on through the hot afternoon. There had been one stroke of luck, the local coal merchant had delivered to quite a few of the villagers in the past week as he usually gave a discount in the summer and a lot of the residents had taken advantage of this.

A couple of times while hurrying through the narrow lanes he nearly came a cropper, tractors backing out of field gates came close to hitting him and a herd of cows going for milking made him stand on the brake pedal for all he was worth. By evening he had given the railway as much as they needed. Maybe tomorrow he could go poaching he thought to himself, at least these days he knew exactly where the Squire was.

Seth had dropped the Morris off at the station and was walking back to his cottage, when he heard the sound of wheels on gravel; the Kind twins drew to a stop beside him in their pre-war Rolls Royce. "Seth, you look worse than the coal man" the twins said in unison.

They were right, his face, arms and clothing were covered with coal dust and his usually white hair was now nearly black. Streaks of sweat from his forehead cut through the grime on his face bearing witness to his exertions. "It's a good job I covered the Squires car seat up, cause it would have been as black as me. I will have to get the old tin bath down when I get in – you ladies off somewhere nice?"

"Just to Mallingford for a stroll through the town, it's such a lovely evening. Good bye Seth." The Rolls drew silently away and Seth walked the last few yards to his cottage.

Sitting at his desk after his evening meal, Reverend Weech stared at the blank sheet of paper before him – next Sunday's sermon. The phone rang and he crossed to the small table it sat on, "I must move the thing to the desk" he thought to himself.

"Hallo! Olly? Olly! My dear old friend – how are you?" Olly Matthews the Bishop of Wellchester had news. "Sam, you are not going to believe it, I think I have found you an engine."

"Olly, by all the saints, are you sure?"

"Yes Sam, I am sure I can get you No 1462, you know the engine

Mr Valentine and Dan... err, borrowed."

"Olly, my dear friend – how?" Mr. Weech sat down on the small stair case by the phone.

"Well I had heard that British Railways decided to get rid of her, she was really hardly damaged at all, only a bit of damage to the Buffer Beam and then, would you believe it, I heard from my friend Arthur that he had just bought her!"

"But Olly, we could not possibly buy her, there's no money, and I'm afraid Mr Valentine will not be forthcoming."

"How is the Insurance coming along?"

"We have the funds from them to lift 1401, and what is left of the carriage, and for repairs, but we won't see any money ourselves."

"I was going to say Sam, you don't need any money – he will lend her to you for the time being, you will have to insure her of course."

"Yes, yes of course! Go on Olly – when?"

"There is only one problem Sam, she's over in Much Abbot – but still on the low loader, all you have to do is go and get her."

"Can we get her here by rail?" Reverend Weech was crossing his fingers.

"I'm sorry Sam, I have been through every possibility with Arthur, but British Railways can't deliver her to us in time."

"Well we are sunk Olly, if we cannot get her here by rail..."

"Sam, Sam, where is your fighting spirit?"

"You don't understand Olly, the Ministry is coming back and they say the agreement for the permanent light railway order can only really apply to the rolling stock we purchased from British Railways."

"Oh, I say Sam."

"Although Mr Clegg tested us using *Thunderbolt*, we are not really allowed to continue the service with our different rolling stock."

"When is he coming?"

"Tuesday week." Reverend Weech said the words with a heavy heart.

"You can do it Sam, of course you can! It would only take a few days to sort out 1462; you know it is a good engine." Olly was trying to boost his old friend.

"Even if we can get her here we shall still need another carriage, fortunately it does not have to be the same as we had, but it cannot be Dan's coach, it must be one built for the purpose."

"Alright Sam, let's solve one problem at a time, who can you send to get 1462?"

"Well we now have Harry Hawkins, you know the roller driver who lent us his driving chain, I'll tell you the whole story later."

"Fine." said Olly, "I will confirm the details with you tomorrow but in the mean time you keep your chin up and tell Hawkins he is off on a trip." After expressing his gratitude to Olly, Sam put his finger on the hand set rest and dialled Gordon's number – perhaps they still had a chance after all.

Harry stood in his usual spot at the bar looking across at Joan. He knew he must tell her his secret if he was to marry her, but he also knew it might break her heart and that there would be no marriage. He stared into his pint, the Reverend Weech and the Squire had both said they would speak for him, and he was her hero again after saving *Thunderbolt* last night…

Reverend Weech and the Squire came sweeping into the Grasshopper, calling for Harry and Dan. "Harry, Dan – we have got a new engine, 1462." Reverend Weech could hardly contain himself.

"Hey, Hey," shouted Dan "did you hear that Mr Valentine, that's our engine that is!"

"Oh, I say!" said Mr Valentine turning to the company "We must all have a drink to celebrate, Padre, Mr Chesterford – your usual?"

"Yes, thank you Mr Valentine, but we must have a word with Harry; unfortunately 1462 is quite a distance away over in Much Abbott." Gordon looked across at Harry, "Can you go and get her for us Harry?"

"Phew, that is quite a way away; it'll take a few days to get her back here."

"We know Harry," countered Reverend Weech, "but the only one who can go and get her is you."

"The trouble is Harry; she has to come by road," Gordon took his pint from Fred, "and we only have eight days."

Harry rubbed his unshaven chin thoughtfully with his left hand, and glanced across at Joan, who was again beaming with pride. "Right you are Reverend, I'll go over on my motor bike, you just tell me when."

More celebratory drinks were ordered, with Dan consuming more than most. Fred forgot the vodka for Dan's last drinks and by last orders he was back to his old ways. Fred and Joan finally got him up to his room, but after they had gone to bed, he crept downstairs again and helped himself to whatever was in the optics. After a mixture of glasses of rum, whisky and brandy Dan could just about move and if he focused his brain he could still see. From the high spirits of the earlier evening his mood had now become very maudlin, he wanted back what he saw every day, and what everyone else used – his home.

Lurching to his feet, Dan weaved his way through the door and out into the night, leaving the pub door wide open once more. How he found his way back to his old coach without breaking his neck is a mystery but he got there. He climbed onto the wagon, opened the coach door, collapsed onto the floor and passed out.

CHAPTER 7

Tuesday

—

One week to inspection

Coming down in the morning poor Fred found the front door wide open, his optics nearly empty and Dan missing. He phoned the Vicar and Squire as a matter of course, and by the time Harry called round on his motor bike he had Dan's clothes packed in a bundle – Dan had been evicted. "When you see the Squire and Vicar, tell them from me that I have had enough, so he is out and his bill is waiting."

Harry nodded, took the bundle and headed off to the station, as Harry passed Pearce and Crump's garage three men came from the side of the building and watched him pass by.

"I think we should have a talk to Harry tonight" said one.

"We don't want to give our game away, I don't want to end up inside" said number two.

The third gazed after Harry "You heard what they were on about in the pub last night, if they get another engine that'll be two we will have to wreck."

The first turned to the others. "We have got to put the frighteners on Hawkins, he has to go for that engine and not come back, or better still wreck it on the journey." Nodding in agreement the three turned towards the heart of the village.

"He's done it again!" exclaimed Joan, holding her nose. Gordon and Harry dragged Dan up from the sofa; put his head out the door, and Reverend Weech poured a bucket of cold water over it. Dan yelled and said words in his native Welsh that they could not understand.

After a half hour he regained some parts of his brain and sat on the edge of the water trough, his eyes trying to focus on the bundle lying at his feet. "Here!" he shouted, and then winced with the pain in his head, "Here, that's my new clothes!"

Joan came to the carriage door and looked out, "Yes they are you old goat and you need a new home too – Dad's chucked you out."

"I have got a home, it's here, and I wants it back."

"Dan, old lad, we know you want it back, but we need it," Reverend Weech looked back from the footplate.

"It is my home. I am sorry Reverend, but I want my home back."

"Alright Dan." Gordon could see the old boy was upset, "we will see what we can do."

"Well all right then." Dan passed his bundle to Gordon, and slowly climbed aboard *Thunderbolt*. When the steam pressure got up *Thunderbolt* rolled into the station to pick up Mr Valentine, Mr Blakeworth, and the locals, it was another beautiful warm and sunny day.

"What is that steam crane doing there, I thought they had finished yesterday evening?" Reverend Weech said, looked across towards the siding.

Just as he has said those words the telephone rang in the office and a couple of seconds later, Emily came to the door. "Reverend, the gentleman who is in charge of that crane over there, says is it alright if he leaves it here for a couple of days?"

"That's fine Emily, tell him it is not in our way – right gentlemen, the road awaits!" Reverend Weech gave a toot on *Thunderbolt*'s whistle and they pulled out on time. As they passed the accident spot, 1401 and most of the carriage had gone. The other part of the carriage was still where it had fallen with one wheel laying farther down the embankment.

"Look!" said Harry, "that's why they left the crane behind that lot is lying in an awkward position – good luck to them getting that lot out."

As the runs progressed during the day, various ideas were sounded out and by the last run back they had a solution – Dan would move into the Station Master's office. His bed was already stored there, they could set it up, and there was running water, a toilet, and electricity. Whilst Harry and Reverend Weech were putting *Thunderbolt* to bed, Gordon was giving the idea an airing with Dan.

"But I still ain't got my home back Squire." Dan stood with his shoulder's drooping.

"Yes I agree Dan, but look at what you have got, a good room, with water and electric."

"Got that at the pub," said Dan.

"Not now you haven't, Fred put you out and we have got to pay your bill. Look if you stay here, and we use your carriage, we will pay you rent again."

Harry, Joan, Reverend Weech and Gordon had Dan's new home sorted in no time. They gave him the key and it was agreed nothing should be said to anyone as to Dan's new abode, security was the watchword.

At eight o'clock that evening Ollie Matthews rang: "Sam, it's all sorted out, all Harry has to do is to get himself there. Arthur has agreed to help get her to you, as I said she is on a transporter, so Harry will be co-driver and they must work out a route that brings them to you avoiding any low bridges."

"Gosh Olly, you are right, one low bridge could spell disaster."

"Good luck Sam, I am trying to find you a carriage, but so far no luck." Sam put the hand set down onto the cradle and smiled.

"Harry!" called Fred over the bar of the Grasshopper, "just had a phone call from the Vicar, could you make sure Dan gets home alright and he says he will tell you about your trip tomorrow."

Joan put her hand on top of Harry's. "I am so proud Harry, everyone is relying on you." Harry smiled at her, he was just plucking up courage to confess his earlier sins when she patted his hand and moved away to serve a customer.

Three men sitting in the corner of the public bar watched and listened.

CHAPTER 8

Wednesday

—

Will Dan ever find a new home?

Wednesday morning, just seven days to go and Dan was actually up, washed (after a fashion) and along at the shed before the others arrived. *Thunderbolt* rolled alongside the platform. "Mornin' Mr Blakeworth, Mr Valentine." called Dan.

"What is wrong with Dan this morning Mr Chesterford?" asked Mr Blakeworth.

As Gordon stepped onto the platform he replied "He's got a new home."

"Where?"

"The Station Master's office."

"He can not" said Mr Blakeworth aghast, "no one can live on what is classed as commercial property."

"What about Station Masters? I know there are Station Masters' houses built into Stations." Gordon was sure he had got things right.

"Ah" Said Mr. Blakeworth, "but Titfield never had the Station Master living here, your Great Grandfather provided a cottage in the village."

"Sam," called Gordon, "we have a problem."

The Vicar descended onto the platform, "I think we have several Gordon."

"It's Dan." said Mr Blakeworth.

"Mr Blakeworth is saying Dan cannot live here at the Station." Gordon was shaking his head as he spoke.

"It is quite true, no matter that this is privately owned, it is still classed as commercial property. Put it this way, if anyone informs the Ministry then we have had it, end of story."

The Reverend Weech looked at his pocket watch. "We must be going; we will have to sort something out this evening." He climbed back aboard

Thunderbolt, Mr Blakeworth entered the carriage with Mr Valentine and Gordon climbed aboard the guards van. "The first thing we must to do when we get to Mallingford is get her coaled up, they will have no excuse as the bill will have been paid." Harry and Dan nodded in agreement. Dan was informed of the new situation as they got *Thunderbolt* rolling.

"What? I've got to move again…..Right; I want my old place back again."

"Dan, Dan, old chap – be reasonable" Reverend Weech was clutching at straws now. "What about if you came to stay with the Squire or myself?"

Dan looked up from his shovelling. "If I stays with you that Emily would have me hymn singing and the Squire would have my shotgun off me – no. Better I go back to my place!" The Vicar gave up, *Thunderbolt* needed all his concentration.

The three men stood outside Pearce and Crump's garage – Alec Pearce's three brothers. They all had Alec's build and hair colouring. The oldest Alistair, the second Fergal, and the third, (who was younger than Alec) Frazer.

Alistair looked at the other two. "We have to do something; our Alec has said there is going to be another inspection on Tuesday."

"They will never last." answered Fergal.

"They might if we don't do something about it!" Frazer was the real hothead of the bunch.

"We could wreck the engine, take something off it – we all know enough about engineering, let's take the steam pressure gauge off." replied Fergal.

"That would stop the thing alright, but they might call the Ministry and say the engine had been vandalised, they told the Inspector that they had been vandalised before."

Alistair started strolling about the site and the others followed. "No, Hawkins is the answer, you heard them – they are sending him for that other engine, what would happen if they did not get it?"

"How's about if we get Hawkins, knock him off that bike of his?" Frazer beamed at the other two.

"Luckily no one's been hurt so far, including you, so let's keep it that way eh? Knock him off his bike – you idiot…" Alistair glowered at Frazer. "Look all we have to do is to have a word with Hawkins, if he doesn't do as he is told we tell his girlfriend," Alistair smiled at his brothers "even if he gets here with an engine they still need a carriage, and they aren't easy to find."

****

The crew was standing on the platform at Mallingford. The Reverend Weech looked at the others. "The question of Dan's home – I think the only thing to do is to remove his coach and replace it."

"What with?" Asked Gordon. "To be honest with you I have not got a clue."

The Reverend Weech had been pondering the problem for most of the day, but then he had a new thought. "The Bedford…."

"Come again Sam?"

"The Bedford!"

Gordon turned to Harry. "Yes, of course, we take Dan's coach off its wagon and put Pearce and Crump's Bedford on instead! What do you say Harry – we can do it, can't we?"

"I suppose we could Squire, but it won't be easy. For a start we will need help – we can't do it all on our own."

"You could use your roller to drag it off." Reverend Weech was getting his teeth into the problem.

"Steady on, steady on, that's my home you are talking about! Drag it and you will have its bottom out – I'll sue you!" Dan's Welsh voice was rising.

Gordon reassured him, "We'll be careful Dan, don't you worry. Our friends from the village will help, your coach will come off easily with the help of Harry's roller and then we can put the Bedford straight on to the flat wagon."

With Dan placated, the Reverend Weech asked if anyone had any other suggestions, and with no response he outlined the plan.

"Right Harry, you drop off when we get back to Titfield and get your roller fired up and ready at the station by the time we're back from our last run. Look out, time to go!"

As *Thunderbolt* and its train approached Titfield station the Reverend Weech looked out on the left side.

"Harry! We might not need your roller if we could get that crane going – what do you say?"

"Yes if I can get it going Reverend, we could come alongside and lift Dan's coach on to the platform. Mind you, we would still have to get it into the yard." Harry strained his eyes checking to see if the crane looked capable of reaching across two tracks. "No, I reckon we will need the roller, we can't expect to move that old carriage with our bare hands."

"Right here is the revised plan." said Reverend Weech "Harry, you get both the crane and your roller fired up, meanwhile Gordon will take his Morris and collect some of our friends from the village to help when we return. Right Dan – let's get her run around and ready for the last trip."

The Reverend Weech waved to Gordon, the passengers alighted, a few more got on and Mr Valentine raised his glass to Joan in Dan's coach.

They rolled back in to Titfield for the last time that day; Harry had got both the fires going. Gordon jumped into the Morris and headed for the village while the Reverend and Dan ran *Thunderbolt* around, finally positioning her at the Mallingford end of the platform. The three of them gathered at the steam crane.

"You ever used one of these things before Vicar?" Harry asked, wiping his hands on a piece of waste before stuffing it back into his pocket.

"Never Harry, she is all yours." Reverend Weech and Harry climbed into the cab of the crane.

"I think I can manage Vicar, I will run her alongside the flat wagon, and there should be enough jib swing to place Dan's coach on to the platform."

"Good for you Harry, we will need some ropes or chains though won't we?" Reverend Weech climbed down from the crane "Ropes, I think – I am sure Seth will have some around here somewhere."

The crane clanked and hissed in protest as Harry moved it into position. Then they lowered the stabilising jacks and tried out the jib alongside the train. Dan was now looking worried, was he was going to get what he wanted? "They will have to pay if they harm my place" he thought to himself.

Gordon returned with enough villagers to do the job, Seth being amongst them.

"Where are you going with her when you gets her on the platform Vicar?" Seth was scratching his head.

"In the station yard Seth – there should be enough room there don't you think?"

"How you going to do that Vicar?" Seth was standing on the platform, looking around.

"We will just…. Ah I see what you mean Seth, there's not enough space to put it down." he answered.

"Those railings will have to go Vicar, and those flower beds." Seth was sizing up the job.

"But Seth, the villagers worked so hard on those beds, it would be such a pity…"

"Tell you what Vicar, we could move the flower beds down the platform a bit, and while this lot are doing that, I will cut a section of the railings out, I can probably make a gate when I put them back." Seth started searching in his tool bag for his hacksaw.

"Alright everybody, if you could start working on the flower beds we will get the move under way. Harry – let's get the ropes in place. They managed to slip two strong hemp ropes that Seth had managed to get hold of under Dan's carriage, and then swung them up over the roof.

Harry climbed up the jib, and reaching over to secure the rope ends together he was then able to attach the ropes to the hook. Getting back into the cab, he juggled the throttle, moving the jib and the crane. It protested, clouds of steam coming from all its joints and all its linkages clanging and banging, but he got it moving where he wanted to and the coach began to lift.

"She's going!" shouted Harry. The gardeners stopped to look, the jib lifted the carriage slowly from the flat bed, Harry gently got the jib to swing towards the station and easing the controls he soon had the carriage clear of the train and held just above the platform's surface. Some of the villagers had gathered sawn up old telegraph poles together and were laying them on the platform, in the direction of the yard. Harry gently lowered Dan's coach onto the rollers with the help of Gordon and Reverend Weech, who helped to guide the carriage onto the rollers.

"Right!" shouted Harry, "I am going to get the roller now, you lot get the ropes off. You got those railings free yet Seth?"

"Just about done Harry, we will be ready in a minute." Seth called back.

Harry got the roller moving towards the railings, ready to pull Dan's carriage into the station yard. Dan himself was eyeing up some old sleepers lying against the embankment.

"Here Reverend, we could put my little place on some of those, not too many mind, I needs a lower step than I had before."

"Good idea Dan – Right gentlemen, if you could lie some of those sleepers down over there…" The Reverend walked through the gap which was now in the railings as Gordon wrapped the rope around Dan's carriage and Harry hooked it back on to the roller.

"Now I will pull back gentle like and if you lot put the rollers down in front, she'll go no bother." Harry climbed back onto the roller. "Now!" he eased the roller back and the villagers placed the poles in front of Dan's place, and it moved slowly into its new position.

"Good people if you could gather round to lift Dan's home onto its new base." The Reverend Weech stood beside Dan as they worked to get it on to its new sleeper base; some wag made a comment about moving Dan's coach becoming a habit, Dan looked around and said it was not his fault. It took a few minutes, but Dan's carriage finally stood firm and level – everyone gave a cheer.

"Well Sam, that's Dan sorted out, are you ready for stage two?" Gordon was looking at the Bedford. "Let Harry get the roller out of the way, and then if you could do the honours and move the Bedford on to the platform, we shouldn't take too long." Reverend Weech walked back towards the platform and explained the next move to the villagers.

Gordon drove the Bedford through the gap they had made in the fence on to the platform, parking it alongside the well wagon facing in the direction of Mallingford. The villagers then moved in to help sling the ropes around the Bedford. Harry had climbed back aboard the crane, and now positioned the jib over the roof of the bus. Seth was helped up on to the roof of the bus and carefully worked to secure the ropes on to the hook.

Once he was helped down, the crane chuffed and clanked in protest as Harry operated the controls to lift the jib and now suspended Bedford off the platform and swing it gently out over the well wagon, and with Gordon and the Reverend guiding he gently lowered it down into place.

"A perfect fit!" Seth waved to Harry and helped one of the villagers up to the roof to release the ropes. "I think we might need a little bridge over this gap here Vicar." Seth said pointing to the gap between the platform and the steps of the bus, "I will fix something up by the morning."

"Oh, well done Seth! And thank you very much everybody, if you would not mind indulging us just a little more we need to chain the bus down, and our task is complete."

"If I take out a couple of seats Vicar, I could put a little bar in to keep our Mr Valentine happy." Seth gave a little grin.

Sam looked at Gordon. "Where is Mr Valentine?"

As the company made its way back into the station yard, Mr Valentine put his head through Dan's carriage window. "I say – I must have dozed off!"

"Come on out Mr Valentine, my old beauty, you missed all the fun!"

K1H731

JW 26/65.

Dan helped Mr Valentine down from his coach, newly positioned on its sleeper base.

"I say Dan, you have been derailed – time we all had a little drink, what?"

"You never mind that Mr Valentine, you're quite right though – time we all had a little drink." Dan slapped him on the back as they set off for the Grasshopper together.

"I have got my home back now!"

Harry was damping down the roller's fire grate, the last of three that busy evening and the villagers were going home after putting the last of Dan's things into his carriage. As he raked the last of the ashes out of the grate he was deep in thought – should he tell Joan tonight or not? His stomach was churning, he hadn't had good night's sleep for ages, the Reverend Weech and the Squire would speak up for him, and they had forgiven his actions against the railway. "I'm sure even Dan would side with me now" he thought "but what about Joan?"

"You going to the pub Harry?" Called out the last helping villagers as they walked past his roller, he heard their feet on the gravel and not looking up waved his arm in acknowledgement. He decided then to go to the pub and act normal, that was the best thing to do – the best way forward, he thought to himself.

"Harry!" Called Joan, as he finally got into the Grasshopper. "Here is your pint, the Reverend and the Squire have been telling me about you got the bus onto the flat wagon after I left!"

Three heads lifted up from their beer as they heard Joan's words and the Pearce brothers exchanged furtive glances one to another. "That settles it – we sort Hawkins out." Alistair lifted his pint and took a slow swig.

"But how?" Asked Fergal.

"That barmaid still doesn't know about Harry and our Alec, so we'll have a word with Harry boy – but if he doesn't play along…….."

CHAPTER 9

Thursday

—

The new carriage

Thursday morning, it was bright, sunny and early – Harry banged on the door of Dan's coach. "Get out of that pit you old devil – come on!" a groan came from inside.

"Oooooh, Harry" came a croaking voice from the interior.

"If you don't get up and out, a bucket of water is coming in," Harry was looking round for a bucket.

"You are cruel Harry Hawkins, cruel – I am getting up!" Dan pushed open the coach door, he appeared bleary eyed and fully dressed including his cap, with a fine padded Burgundy dressing gown over the top.

"I don't believe it!" Harry looked at Dan in his finery.

"What?" Dan gave Harry one of his glowering looks, "Do you expect me to go across to my bathroom, without the proper ati ati…. the proper clothes on?"

"Bathroom? It was not so long ago all you had was a bucket, now get a move on, I'm going to get *Thunderbolt* lit up – don't be long." Dan moved muttering to himself, as he went to his ablutions.

Harry was getting her nicely fired when Seth strolled by, tool bag swung over his shoulder. "Seth, don't you ever sleep?" asked Harry resting on his shovel.

"You get plenty of sleep when you are dead… I'll have a nice snooze in the garden this afternoon so I will – I'm off!"

"Good on yer Seth." Harry shovelled on.

Dan and Reverend Weech arrived together. "Oh good show Harry! I've just seen Seth, he said he'd put another temporary bar into the bus and that he's made a bridge."

Thunderbolt headed out of the shed, with an even more bizarre train than usual. The three Pearce Brothers, leaning on the crossing gate, watched and stared at Harry as he passed, shaking their heads as Alec's pride and joy passed by chained onto the flat wagon.

"I say! I say!" called Mr Valentine, "Bravo, my dear friends, bravo!"

"Wait until we put the bridge across Mr Valentine" shouted Harry, and swung down to lift the broad planks across from the platform to the bus steps.

"You first Joan my dear" Mr Valentine held Joan's hand as she stepped up into the bus.

"Oh, Mr Valentine" Joan exclaimed, "Seth has done you proud again!"

"Gosh!" Mr Valentine whispered, "A veritable miracle Joan – who could imagine it, a bus on a train with a bar."

"That's another first for the Titfield Railway!" Joan squeezed behind the bar that Seth had put in at the back of the bus – he had to remove four sets of seats to accomplish the task.

Mr Blakeworth came aboard followed by the morning locals. "You know Joan; it was surely a waste of time for poor old Seth to go to all this trouble for maybe only a few days." Mr Blakeworth sat at the front of the bus.

"My dear Mr Blakeworth." Mr Valentine picked up his Gin and Tonic. "Firstly, Seth could never waste his time on such a noble project, and how could we spoil our fine tradition by allowing a train of ours to travel without its greatest achievement, to wit – a bar."

Mr Blakeworth shook his morning paper, "greatest achievement indeed!"

The Squire blew his whistle and *Thunderbolt* drew out of the station.

The Mallingford signal box window was open to catch a breeze to cool down the box, the bell sounded for a train entering their section. "Listen" said Taff "that is the *Thunderbolt*!" As the train drew into view Taff's jaw dropped. "Ernie come and take a look at this – they are giving a bus a piggy back!"

Ernie was busy picking out his horses on the racing page and was not interested.

"Taff if you said that they were coming up on that Squire's old Corvette, I would say drop the signal and let them through."

Mallingford people waiting for *Thunderbolt* on the station were taken aback by her unusual coach, but the enthusiasts, although wanting to travel behind *Thunderbolt*, could not bring themselves to board it. Most of them stood on the platform to admire the old engine and stayed behind, with only a few travelling back to Titfield.

So a sunny Thursday passed and between *Thunderbolt's* increasing clanks and wheezing they even heard the birds sing. They got more onlookers than usual as they went back and forth with their new coach; in fact the over bridges were packed with school children, waving at the unusual sight after they had finished for the day.

Emily and Sally (who had been helping out) stood on the platform as they pulled in on the last run of the day, Emily waited until the last passengers had given their tickets up before calling Reverend Weech. "The Bishop has been on the phone for you Mr Weech. Says he thinks he might have found us a carriage – can you call him?"

"I say, did you hear that Gordon, a carriage! It will be like starting all over again."

"And so it shall Sam, we will show them – you in a 1400 tank again and me with a real carriage in front of the brake van!"

"If you can see to *Thunderbolt* Gordon, I'll go and phone the Bishop – meet you in the Grasshopper this evening."

"Padre wait, I'll walk with you." Mr Valentine hurried after Reverend Weech.

Gordon waved Reverend Weech over to the table where he and Mr Valentine were sitting, Dan and Harry were propping up the bar within earshot. "Cheers!" Said Reverend Weech sipping his sweet sherry, "I think everything has been settled. I am sorry I have not consulted you both but time has been of the essence."

"Come on Padre, tell us the good news." Mr Valentine inched his chair closer to the table.

"Olly Matthews received a phone call this morning, it seems there were a few carriages up for sale, some were only fit for the scrap yard, but some were still in very good condition and had good bogies." He took another sip of his sherry. "A friend of his bought one, it used to be a third class restaurant car, built at Doncaster in 1909, he says it has a bar, a small kitchen and a toilet. I don't expect it will be in showroom condition, but we can sort it out – it was last used by the LNER. Oh I nearly forgot, it has tables and chairs and we can have it on loan until we find a carriage of our own!"

"Oh Sam, well done….. Miss Hampton dear, – same again!" Mr Valentine waved at Joan.

The Reverend continued. "Now this kind gentleman has given us the carriage on extended loan, he is planning to use it as a camping van, but he also told Olly he will try and get another one for us to use permanently – it seems you can get them if you know where to look."

"That will be fine Sam, the Insurance will pay for it, and you never know, we might manage enough for a second one." Gordon emptied his pint glass as Joan arrived with the drinks.

"There is only one problem though; the carriage won't be at Mallingford until late Monday night. It is coming to us via a series of 'lifts' – that's the reason for the delay."

"Could we get it any sooner?" Asked Mr Valentine.

"The cost of it coming in one journey would be prohibitive, we could not afford it. By way of good fortune Olly's friend just happens to work for British Railways and can arrange a series of shorter journeys on ordinary trains." Reverend Weech waved Dan and Harry over and told them of the situation.

"That's alright Mr Weech; we will have 1462 on Monday so Dan and I can run light to Mallingford, wait in the sidings, and bring the carriage down ready for Tuesday morning."

They all raised their glasses. "To The Titfield Railway Company!"

They were being watched from the public bar…

CHAPTER 10

Friday

—

Poor Harry

Friday started out well, it was another warm and sunny day and the valley was looking at its best. Ron and Sally were helping out, so Gordon had company in the guard's van and Sally worked with Emily after the morning rush (at least ten passengers) to get down to a bit of station cleaning ready for the Ministry Inspection. A hard brushing and a bucket of water saw the soil marks from the old flower bed gone and by midday the station looked a treat, with the flower baskets watered and blooming and even the toilets sparkling after Dan's recent use, all ready for inspection.

On the track *Thunderbolt* was giving cause for concern, there seemed to be a slight knock coming somewhere from her running gear. They took turns leaning out over the side listening intently, trying to trace the source. After the mid day trip Dan, Reverend Weech, Gordon, and Ron stood beside the track as *Thunderbolt* ran round the train, they hoped running light would make it easier to locate the source of the noise. They listened, but they could not pin the location down. Dan and Reverend Weech went round every oiling point and felt every bearing to see if they were running hot – nothing!

Mr Valentine was quietly drinking at the bar whilst Joan was preparing a light lunch of sandwiches for herself and her permanent customer. "I am out to a function on Monday evening Joan, should be quite a splendid affair. Of course Mrs Valentine won't be attending, I don't know why but she does not seem to like some of my friends."

"Really, Mr Valentine?" smiled Joan, "And do your friends like a good evening?"

"My dear Joan, of course, we all like a little libation, it simply would not be a good evening otherwise."

"Mallingford is it?"

"Ah, yes. I'm afraid I will be away from my usual haunts, but still, it will take my mind of that Ministry walla."

Joan finished making the sandwiches. "There you are Mr Valentine, you know my poor Harry has to make his own sandwiches."

"Ah, yes my dear, but one fine morning after the nuptials, they will be made for him by your own sweet hand."

"Well that's as it maybe, Mr Valentine, but we need to make more profit before Harry and I can get wed, I should say we both need a pay rise."

"My dear that you shall, what must you be thinking of me, by Jove, you must both have a pay rise at once?"

"But Mr Valentine, the company……"

"Nonsense my dear girl, why, I will gladly pay out of my own pocket, and Dan must have a rise too."

"Oh, Mr Valentine!" Joan reached across the counter and kissed Mr Valentine on his left cheek.

"Joan my dear, I think that calls for another little drink, pray join me as I toast you and Harry."

Their afternoon passed pleasantly, both were quite tipsy by the last run and unaware of the others' concern for *Thunderbolt*. After they had put her back in the shed, *Thunderbolt* was oiled and checked over again.

The crew walked back to the station together, Dan went to his coach and Harry stood at the Morris with Gordon and Reverend Weech. "I should tell her, I really should, but every time I get enough courage up I stop myself – what if she won't forgive me? I know I have done some terrible things."

"But Harry, you have done a lot of good things since. You have saved *Thunderbolt*, given up well paid work for us – you could not have done more!" Reverend Weech patted Harry on the shoulder.

"It's fair churning me up, and no mistake." Harry shook his head.

"We will stand by you Harry," said Gordon trying to sound positive, "If you think you are going to tell her, tip us the wink, and we will be right beside you – right Sam?"

"Of course! Of course! Harry, I want nothing better than to pronounce you and Joan Man and Wife myself!" Heartened, Harry said goodbye and started up his bike. Gordon gave Reverend Weech a lift up to the Vicarage in the Morris.

Harry was coming round the tight bend at the top of the village, just by

Pearce and Crump's garage, when three men stepped out into the road in front of him. "Here, watch it." Harry braked sharply, nearly coming off his bike, the engine was still racing.

"Steady now, you nearly had an accident then – would be a pity that." Alistair Pearce was standing directly in front of Harry. "We hear you're going for that engine tomorrow."

"Yes – so what?" Harry was feeling uneasy.

"It would be a very good idea if you didn't get back with it until after Tuesday." Frazer spat the words out.

"And why is that?" Harry glowered back at them.

"No engine or carriage – no railway after Tuesday, but if we tell that girlfriend of yours about you and Alec then you won't have her to come back to. Alistair smiled at Harry.

"You might have that wrong, who says I haven't told her already?" Harry tried a smile of triumph, and hoped he had got away with it.

"Alright, let's put it another way Hawkins, whether she knows or not, if our Alec changes his story then you are in it up to your neck – so don't come back with that engine." Alistair nodded at Harry slowly.

"Or else!" butted in Frazer.

"Think about it Hawkins…but if you are late back with the engine, then Alec will keep you out of it." Alistair stepped aside.

With petrol fumes whispering from the engine, Harry revved up the bike and went on his way.

At eight o'clock he was back at the Grasshopper. No celebrating tonight, he sat with Gordon and the Reverend Weech, telling them of his journey home. "What am I going to do? I'm done for, no Joan, no job – only jail!"

"Steady Harry, we are not done for yet." The Reverend Weech sat closer to the table.

"No, but I am," Harry took a hasty look around "they are over in the public bar watching, they will know what we are talking about."

"Then we must call their bluff Harry – we must all laugh out loud and you wave at Joan as if you have not got a care in the world."

"But…"

"Don't think about it – just do it now." They all roared with laughter, Joan looked across at them and Harry waved, Joan returned his wave with the tea towel she used for drying the glasses and blew Harry a kiss. Mr Valentine ordered another round of drinks, at which Dan cheered.

"See," whispered Reverend Weech, "not a care in the world – that will show them!"

"They might try something else though Sam." Gordon looked across at the three sullen faces.

"I think they have swallowed Harry's story about telling Joan and hopefully they now know that Harry has told us about their threat." Reverend Weech now looked across the bar. "It is all we can do for now. It might be an idea though Harry that when you get back with 1462 you put her on the line at the colliery crossing – we don't want them getting their hands on her."

"Time we all had a drink!" Said Mr Valentine, putting a tray with two pints and a sherry on the table.

CHAPTER 11

Saturday

—

Harry's journey

Saturday morning: All the plans had been made in the Grasshopper the previous evening, Harry was ready to travel to Much Abbott for 1462 on his motorbike, checking the route as he went. After staying the night with Arthur Grout, he and Arthur would check 1462 over Sunday and then bring her back on Monday. Harry called round to the Grasshopper to see Joan, after giving her a lift to the station he set off on his journey.

Much Abbott was one hundred and forty five miles away and the old bike was not as fast as it used to be, but the weather held and at last he was on his way. Harry had to remember one important thing, to check the height of every bridge he went under. Arthur Grout had estimated the height of 1462 to be seventeen feet, from the top of the chimney to the ground including the transporter, and with that in mind Harry travelled north.

He was hoping to find the most direct route, so the height of the bridges was essential knowledge. At lunchtime Harry called into a village pub standing next to a wide green. A couple of rounds of home cured ham sandwiches and a pint went down a treat, but Harry could not afford to waste time. As he passed through small villages and country towns, the Pearce Brothers threat echoed in his mind, it broke his concentration a little but he still managed to note the height of the bridges as he passed underneath them.

Whilst Harry was travelling to Much Abbott, back on the railway *Thunderbolt* was giving more cause for concern, the noise they could not quite trace was getting louder. At every opportunity they checked her for hot bearings, and oiled her running and driving gear, at Titfield, Mallingford, and even at the Water Tower. Yes, some of the bearings were running a little warm, but then it was a hot day.

As they rolled out of Mallingford on their final run of the day Reverend Weech made a decision. "We will have to rest her tomorrow Dan – if we continue running her we might do irreparable damage and what would the museum say then?"

"But what about tomorrow's service – we have to provide transport don't we?"

"I know you are right Dan, but what choice do we have? We could say that the track has to have vital repairs."

"What if the Ministry in London finds out?" Plenty of Pearce and Crump spy's about – they could check the track easy enough."

"I will ask the Squire and Mr Valentine when we get to Titfield." Sam eased the regulator and nursed *Thunderbolt* along.

Back at Titfield and with all the passengers gone, Dan climbed down and checked *Thunderbolt* for the umpteenth time that day. Reverend Weech called The Squire and Mr Valentine on to the platform. "We will have to rest her tomorrow and check her bearings, which means dismantling her running gear and that will take all day – even if we don't find anything."

"This is serious Sam, we must run a service – the Ministry could take away our license."

"Oh Padre, say this is not the end, we cannot fail now!"

"I know Mr Valentine, but what else can we do? If we damage her not only will we lose the railway, but the Museum could sue us for any damage done and we are not insured for that."

"Oh I say," Mr Valentine was chief shareholder and he would have to bear the expense.

"Yes Mr Weech you are quite right."

"What if we used our cars?" Gordon could think of no other course of action.

"I say Squire – a stroke of genius! Of course I will not be able to drive myself you understand, but Mrs Valentine would do it I am sure."

"The two cars should be enough; we don't usually have many passengers on a Sunday."

Gordon was smiling broadly.

"Licenses." Said the Reverend, glumly.

"Licenses, what do you mean Sam?"

"License and Insurance, both would be required if we were to run a taxi service – that's the law I am afraid."

"Well it is a damn poor law if you ask me. What if we don't charge?" Gordon looked at his partners and waited.

"Yes by jove, well done again Squire! It will be of little cost to the company and we will still be serving our community, who can argue with that?" Mr Valentine was beaming, and he gave a little skip. "Get a move on Dan and get her into the shed, it's time for a little celebration!" He gave another little skip and taking his trilby off waved it above his head. "See you later in the Grasshopper – I am off to tell my good lady about her adventure tomorrow." Mr Valentine turned and away.

"Adventure?" Asked Reverend Weech.

Mr Valentine turned towards them. "Every time my lady wife drives it is an adventure – have you seen the state of the Rover's bumpers?" He was laughing as he went on his way.

"Can't be helped Sam, I am sure we will do just fine." Gordon wondered just what the morning would bring.

It was early evening when Harry arrived at Much Abbott; he wearily climbed off the bike, bending his body backwards with his hands on his hips to ease the pain in his back. Arthur Grout came out of his house and shook hands with Harry. "How was the trip, did you come across any low bridges?"

"Yeh, a couple – do you have a good map?" Asked Harry.

"Yes, pretty good. I have been asking a couple of hauliers for routes back to Titfield, and I think I might have found us a route close to the one you would have travelled today. Anyway, come inside and have something to eat." The two men walked up the gravel path into the imposing farmhouse. Arthur' wife Doris stood at the doorway and welcomed Harry inside.

After Harry had freshened up, and they had eaten their meal and had a drink, Arthur and Harry walked into the yard to inspect the new engine, 14XX tank number 1462, the very same engine that Dan and Mr Valentine had earlier "borrowed" from British Railways. "She looks good." Said Harry.

"Aye she is that – she will be a good solid engine for you, there was not much damage caused – just her buffer beam bent a little. I don't know why they got rid of her; she is good for many years yet."

"I am just glad you are letting us have her, it is going to be a few months before the repairs are completed on our engine and the *Thunderbolt* is having a bit of bother, all of us are worried about her." Harry climbed up onto the footplate of 1462, he opened the firebox door and looked inside – there was just enough evening light in which to see everything. The locomotive was standing on the trailer of a large American tank transporter. "You got this lot ready to go?" he asked, looking down at the unfamiliar tractor unit.

"Yes – it's all set up for our journey. I've also coaled up 1462 and filled her boiler with water, ready for you when we get back to Titfield." Arthur stood and looked up at Harry.

"Don't tell me I might have a day off tomorrow?" Harry smiled.

"Well I hope so, the only worry is that this tractor unit is acting up a bit, but she should do us alright to Titfield." Arthur patted one of the vehicle's large tyres.

"Great, now all we need now is a good pub." smiled Harry, climbing down.

"Got better than that lad, got my own home brew – blow your head off it will!"

"Make sure you don't drink too much." said Doris, who had walked out from the farmhouse "Otherwise you might miss Sunday all together."

CHAPTER 12

Sunday

—

The Bedford on the iron road

Reverend Weech hurried down to the station in the warm morning sunshine. He had been on the phone to Olly Matthews yesterday evening, who had managed to contact an old railway fitter and had arranged for him to come up to Titfield this morning to have a look at *Thunderbolt* – he could be a great help to them. Reverend Weech reckoned he would be able to stay a few hours with him before getting back to his church. He had really spent far too long away from his church duties, but his curate had performed sterling work in his absence. Good old Emily had written out a poster yesterday evening, which was now up on the station gate; it stated NO TRAINS TODAY.

Gordon and Dan were already down at the shed. "Mr Weech, this is Albert, our engineer." Gordon made the introductions.

"How do you do Mr Weech? I have had a quick look and the best things to do are disconnect the driving rods and check the bearings, if there is any wear that is where we are going to find it."

"Please carry on Albert, we are happy to do whatever you suggest."

Albert started work, slackening locking nuts ready to pull the bearings out. It took a while before the driving rods were off, Albert looked for wear and found the problem, and one of the bearing brasses had run its white metal. "There it is gentlemen, it is a good job you stopped running her – that would have damaged her motion. It'll take a bit of time to repair and we will need a machine shop for the job too."

"I can only stay a few minutes longer Albert, what can we do now?" Asked Reverend Weech.

"Find another engine." came Albert's reply.

"There should be another one here tomorrow." Gordon said, "But it will not be here soon enough."

Dan looked back along the track to their train. "We could just use the bus!" he said.

"Dan we cannot use the bus, we need a PSV license, insurance and a qualified driver to run that Bedford on the road with passengers." Gordon shook his head.

"Maybe not on the road, but what about on the track?" said Albert.

"On the track?" Reverend Weech was beginning to think his silent prayer might be answered.

"I have heard they put cars and Lorries on the tracks during the war, and the LMS did something similar with a road coach up at Stratford – I think it might work." Albert was now examining the Bedford. "We take the wheels off, and put wheels on from – but from where?" He scratched his chin thoughtfully.

"What about those permanent way trolley wheels? They look to be about the right size – what do you think?" Asked Dan. "Hmmm, but how are we going to get the Bedford off its wagon?"

Gordon cut in "Harry used the crane to get it on, together with a bit of help from the villagers…."

Just then a car horn beeped and Mr and Mrs Valentine swept in to the yard in their Rover.

"Valentine!" shouted Gordon "we need your car to pull the train!"

"I say old boy, can't expect her to pull the train all the way to Mallingford – she'll get all shook up!"

"No, not to Mallingford – just a short move here in the station." Gordon replied.

"First thing to do is to get the crane fired up; it will take a couple of hours at least. If Harry Hawkins can handle it, then so can I!" Dan looked determined.

"If you think you can do it Dan – then go to it." Gordon went over to Mr Valentine. "We need to move the train along the platform so we can lift the Bedford off the flat wagon and on to the platform by the gate."

"Did you hear that Felicity? You are going to pull the train."

"Oh what fun!" came Felicity's reply, and she restarted the Rover. "Open up the crossing gates for me Walter."

"I say, steady on old girl – you know what you are like in confined spaces."

Dan thought for a moment. "You will need to take the gate right off, and you'll need everyone for that – here Vicar, Squire, Albert – Mr Valentine needs a hand, I've got to go and get that crane started." So saying he set off for the siding where the crane was standing. With even Mr Valentine deigning to help, the gate was soon lifted clear and moved out of the way.

"What is the plan?" asked Mr Valentine.

"Dan says it will take a couple of hours to get steam up, If we pull the train into the station and stop with the wagon just beside the gate, he will be able to pull alongside on the other track and lift the Bedford off and on to the platform."

Mrs.Valentine manoeuvred the Rover round onto the track, the Rover's steering wheel bucked and jumped as she crossed the tracks, but she managed to get it into position. A tow rope was connected and with the Rover's engine straining and the rope taught she managed to get the train moving. With the train rolling Gordon applied the van's brake to bring it to a stand in position for the lift. "Well done, old girl!" Mr Valentine congratulated his wife.

Dan could be heard banging and clattering in the crane's cab while Albert studied the trolley wheels that they proposed attaching to the Bedford. "These will do, let's get them off while Dan is raising steam on the crane. I'll need a hand though, these things are heavy."

Albert, Sam and Gordon started to remove the wheels, Mr Valentine walked over to the Rover, casually glancing at the Rover's body work. "You did very well my dear, maybe just a shade too many revs but all in all a grand job."

"Oh, thank you Walter, now what are we going to do next?" Felicity was ready for the next challenge.

Albert called over to them. "Take the car back over to the station yard; it will be out of the way there."

"Right you are!" Felicity Valentine started up the Rover "Am I clear Walter, is the rope off?"

"Yes my dear, but remember, you have to reverse this time back to where you started from, on the level crossing."

"Walter you are such an old fusspot – off I go!" The Rover's gearbox crunched as reverse gear was found, the car jumped as the gear engaged, and she was off. With the recent praise still ringing in her ears, she could do anything, the car bumped back down the line towards the level crossing and stopped beside the three men standing there.

"I say, can I help you?" She asked pleasantly.

"Where's the train? There should be a train, what's this about no trains?" Alistair asked grumpily.

"That's right; if you want to go to Mallingford today we will take you there in a car for no charge."

"What's this all about lady?" Alistair moved closer to the car.

"Look, I think I might have to do a bit more towing first, so hang on here for a couple of minutes and then I'll gladly take you." Felicity revved the engine, crashed the gears, and ran the Rover straight into the gatepost.

"Woops," trilled Felicity "think I had better stay here!"

"Do you fancy going in that car with her?" asked Fergal.

"That's not the point; there should be a train and not a car."

After a struggle, they got all four wheels off the permanent way trolley. "If we can get these stud holes to line up we are home and dry," Albert was carefully measuring them.

"Thing is though, I think these holes might have to be reamed out to fit over the studs on the Bedford's axles."

The Vicar looked at his pocket watch. "Oh dear, looks like the poor curate will have to do without me again."

"Hi!" shouted Dan, "This crane is getting a good bit of pressure up – won't be long now."

The Pearce brothers were still standing by the station entrance. "If you still want to go to Mallingford I can take you now." Felicity Valentine smiled across at them. The Pearce brothers thought better of it and retreated towards the village.

A while later and with enough pressure up, Dan slowly moved the crane into gear and moved off the siding. He waved for someone to go and change the points. The Reverend Weech ran to lever frame and changed the points, allowing Dan to draw out on to the main line clear of the loop. As Dan put the crane into reverse he changed the points again, allowing the crane to push the well wagon into position on the level crossing.

"Hallo Vicar!" Seth called out; he had been to church (unlike Reverend Weech) and had come down to the station to see if he could be of help.

"Good to see you Seth! You are just in time – we are about to take the Bedford off the flat bed.

"What for?" Asked Seth.

"Why, we're going to run the Bedford on the rails!" Cut in Mr Valentine.

"Ask a daft question," muttered Seth to himself.

"Come on you lot, get those ropes round that Bedford!" Dan clanked alongside the well wagon in the crane. Coming to a stand they lowered the jacks and he gently swung the crane jib out over the Bedford. Seth was assisted on to the roof of the Bedford once again and carefully fixed the ropes from around the coach on to the hook of the crane. "Ready?" shouted Dan. At a nod from Seth, now safely back on the platform, Dan set the flywheel going and the crane slowly started to lift the bus.

"Chains!" Seth suddenly shouted – they were still shackling the Bedford to the wagon.

"Have I got to do every ruddy thing myself?" Dan shouted back as he grappled with the controls to stop the crane lifting any further.

"Hold her there, I'll get them off!" Seth got on to the wagon and pulled the chains free, "Now Dan, lift away!"

Wheezing and coughing, the crane slowly raised the bus and swung it back above the road of the level crossing, so that the Bedford could be placed back down onto the rails on the level crossing, where they would be able to change the wheels. Coming to a stand, Dan gently lowered the Bedford on to the track with Seth and Gordon guiding it into final position. Everyone cheered – they had done it! Dan waved happily from the crane's cab.

Dan and the crane clanked away, through the points and then back to the siding they had come from. The crane was losing pressure; Dan wondered if that was why the railway workers had left it there for so long. He shook his head and returned to the others. "Bad news Reverend – that crane's just about had it. We won't get any more work out of it today."

"Ah well, I think it could just have been a little miracle that it lasted so long, Providence brought it to us just when we needed it!" The Reverend looked skyward with a smile on his face.

"If you says so, you being a man of the cloth and all that – but don't we need it now?" Dan removed his cap and scratched his head. They all stood by the Bedford, Albert measured the distance between the wheels and confirmed that it matched the gauge of the rails; all they needed to do was to change the wheels over.

"We need to lift the bus, but now you say the crane can't lift it – what now?" Gordon said what the others were thinking.

"A big car jack or two would do it, you know, you can drag them about." said Seth.

"But we haven't got one Seth" replied Gordon.

"I have though; I've got two of them! They were out at Pearce and Crump's garage, I lent them to Alec, but I got them back while you were getting the Bedford, before the Police locked the place up. They are in the station store room, didn't Emily tell you?"

"Bless you Seth! Bless you! What would we ever do without you?" Reverend Weech patted him on the back appreciatively.

They set to work, the jacks were placed under the bus and the front wheels removed. They checked the hub studs against the rail wheels, with a little drilling the wheels would fit. "Mallingford engine sheds, that's where we will have to take them – we need a heavy drill for this job." Albert had the job weighed up.

"These wheels are heavy Albert; my Morris might take two, but not four. Gordon looked at Reverend Weech for inspiration.

"Well if Mrs Valentine could take two and you can manage two, then we are in business!" he replied. Felicity Valentine readily agreed and after the wheels were loaded, the two cars set out for Mallingford sheds.

Mr Valentine, the Reverend, Seth, and Dan, walked over to Dan's coach for a well earned cup of tea. "You know Dan," Said Reverend Weech sitting on the bench in front of Dan's old coach, "those men look familiar."

"Seen them in the Grasshopper." Replied Dan.

"Yes – but they remind me of someone." Reverend Weech pondered.

"I wonder how Harry's doing." Dan pulled on a fresh pipe.

"Better than we are, I hope." Reverend Weech sighed.

"Oh he will be doing splendidly, absolutely splendidly I am sure, here – have some of this." and so saying Mr Valentine poured a tot of Whisky into their mugs of tea.

Dan belched noisily.

It took a couple of hours before the cars returned. "Let's hope my measurements are correct." said Albert, as he got out of the Rover and opened the boot to get the two wheels out. Seth and Dan helped him carry the first wheel over to the Bedford, after jacking the coach up they removed the road wheel and offered the first wheel up, the new holes fitting perfectly over the hub studs at the first attempt. After letting the jack down, making sure the flange of the railed wheel dropped inside rail, they moved around the other three wheels of the Bedford repeating the process until the Bedford stood on the rails.

Seth climbed aboard and using stout rope tightly lashed the steering wheel so that the front wheels were locked in a straight ahead position. "There you are Squire, your carriage awaits!" Gordon climbed into the bus, started the engine, and the Bedford moved along the railway line under its own power for the first time.

"I won't tell you the problems we had at the sheds," said Albert, "but all's well that ends well."

"I say, I think a celebratory drink is in order" said Mr Valentine, reaching for the whisky bottle outside Dan's coach.

Felicity Valentine parked just inside the station yard, ready to transport any would be passengers to Mallingford. A few people had turned up later in the afternoon, but seeing no engines had declined her offer and gone away. After the hustle and bustle of the morning the afternoon was a bit of an anti-climax, but the lack of trains and the unexpected time off that it had given the Reverend Weech meant that he could write a new sermon and take Evensong. Meanwhile Dan had a chance to sit outside his coach and contemplate the challenges of the last few days and hours, stretching out in the warm July sunshine he pushed his cap over his eyes and fell into a deep contented sleep.

While all this work had been going on in Titfield, Harry and Arthur had started Sunday rather later than they had intended. They had drunk long and hard after Harry's arrival and in the morning their heads had thundered and thumped. After an unproductive morning, late afternoon had finally seen them stagger into the yard. "She looks OK to me," said Arthur, his mouth still tasting like the inside of his boot.

"Yeah, fine." mumbled Harry, they staggered back into the house for coffee.

CHAPTER 13

Monday

—

Harry heads for home

The next morning in Titfield was rather more relaxed than usual for the train crew and they had all enjoyed a bit of a lie in – you don't have to stoke up a Bedford like a steam engine! The Squire swung aboard; Dan sat at the back next to Mr Valentine's bar, whilst Reverend Weech stood on the platform with Joan. "I do hope Harry will be setting off soon – he's got quite a trip, and I do hope he took careful notice of bridge heights" said Reverend Weech.

"I am sure he has Mr Weech – I'm sure he won't let you down." Joan checked the bottles she had brought in a crate from the pub.

"Harry didn't mention anything to you before he left, did he Joan?"

"What do you mean Mr Weech, about what?" Joan looked up from her bottles.

"Oh, nothing dear, I just wondered, that's all."

Mr Valentine arrived with Mr Blakeworth and the other first trip regulars. "There you are gentlemen! I told you – and there she is." Mr Valentine waved his arm towards the Bedford.

"Well I never" said Mr Blakeworth "I wouldn't have believed it if I hadn't seen it for myself!"

"It happens the entire time dear fellow, all over the world now. Buses on railway tracks and the internal combustion engine, it's going to be the future – mark my words." Mr Valentine seemed to have become the font of all knowledge regarding this latest development on their railway.

"All aboard every one!" Called Reverend Weech. "We have our time table to keep to."

Gordon had the Bedford ticking over, so when everyone was seated, he put her in gear and let out the clutch, and the bus moved smoothly out of the station towards Mallingford. As they passed through the familiar countryside, people already accustomed to the unusual antics of the new railway company stared in disbelief as the Bedford motored past, its gearbox whining and the wheels making an unfamiliar rhythm across the rail joints.

As they approached Mallingford's home signal, Ernie slid back the window of the signal box and looked up the line towards Titfield. "Taff – you are not going to believe this!"

"What now?" said Taff lifting his fresh pot of tea.

"The train now approaching is – a bus!"

"There cannot be a bus on our rails – will you stop messing about." Taff walked towards Ernie and the open window.

"Titfield…." was the only word Ernie could manage. Taff pushed past Ernie and looked out of the window, just as the blue and cream Bedford pulled up outside the box waiting for the signal to drop.

"Hoy!" Shouted Taff.

The door window slid open and the Squire looked out "Can I be of assistance?"

Now the one person from Titfield that Taff actually admired was Gordon Chesterford, the Squire. He had been Captain of a Corvette in the recent hostilities, and had seen a lot of action. "How are you Squire? Not your usual transport eh?"

Ernie sneered behind Taffs back. "Crawler…" he muttered to himself.

"The old *Thunderbolt* is a bit worse for wear at the moment Taff; we need an alternative mode of transport for a few days." The Squire smiled up at Taff.

"Right you are Squire, and how is the family?"

"They're fine Taff, my wife is her usual self and the twins are going on four now."

"That's good to hear Squire, nice to know that everything is going well – I will just drop this signal, and you can be on your way." Gordon waved, he revved the engine and letting out the clutch the Bedford moved away towards the platform and journey's end.

"I noticed you didn't give him any trouble." said Ernie, eying Taff through narrowed eyes from over his mug of tea.

"Now look; that Dan is an old soak, that Vicar is church while I am Chapel, and Harry is no better than he should be – but I will not have

a word said against the Squire, an officer and a gentleman is what he is!"

"Suit yourself Taff, but just wait until they come back." Ernie was chuckling.

"Why?" Taff asked.

"Because they will be going to Titfield backwards!"

"Sam!" Called Gordon. "We will have to travel backwards – we cannot turn the bus round."

"We couldn't turn the engines round either." Growled Dan"

"You know Dan, traveling in reverse all the way back to Titfield might cause some damage," Gordon looked back up the bus; Mr Valentine sipped his Gin and Tonic.

"Don't worry, Dan will look out the back window for you, won't you Dan?"

"Course – ready when you are Squire!" he stood braced in the aisle at the rear of the Bedford ready for departure. Gordon shrugged his shoulders, put the Bedford in to reverse, and they started back for Titfield. As the day progressed taking the bus forward to Mallingford was fine, but returning in reverse was not as easy. Only having the one gear ratio to use it was harder to keep to time and they worried that they might be damaging the gearbox, but then again it was only going to be for the one day.

Arthur kissed his wife goodbye and climbed up into the cab. Harry was already sitting in the passenger seat with a map spread open, studying their route. "Well Harry my old mate, are you ready to go?" Arthur smiled across at Harry.

"I hope this big Yank machine of yours will get us there."

Arthur patted the olive green metal of the dashboard. "She should Harry boy, mind you we had better keep an eye on the four wheel drive." Arthur crashed the gear in and the American White truck jumped forward, the diesel engine roared and they pulled out of the farm gates in a cloud of dust. The one thing they had managed to do on Sunday after their heads cleared was to plan their route, taking into account Harry's knowledge of the various bridge heights on the way.

As they travelled slowly through the countryside thoughts of having to confess to Joan came back into Harry's head, but he concentrated on his map and their route – they couldn't afford to make any mistakes with the huge load of 1462 travelling behind them. Sitting up high in the cab they got a good view of the road ahead and could see over the top of the hedges which lined the roads.

Sometimes they had to slow to a crawl as they passed under low telephone lines, Harry leaning out of the cab to lift clear any cables they thought might snag on 1462 and her tall chimney and dome. The sun was shining on another perfect July day and the countryside was at its best, they were tempted a couple of times to stop at a welcoming pub for a cool pint, but they managed to press on.

At lunch time they came to a pub with a large plot of waste ground just to one side, an ideal spot to park up. A quiet pint with their lunch was interrupted by the local school children wanting to climb aboard 1462, and Harry had to issue a few threats before the children eventually gave up and went back into school.

Time was pressing so they set off again as soon as they had finished their lunch, with Harry now driving for the next leg of the journey. Even though their route was carefully planned, every time they came to a bridge they slowed down, making sure they got 1462's chimney in the dead centre of the road before proceeding.

"You didn't phone your Vicar yesterday Harry – I bet they think we should be arriving about now!" Arthur shouted above the noise in the cab.

"We'll do all right Arthur; we should still get there by about eight o'clock. They will be pleased to see us, don't you worry." Harry suddenly jammed on the brakes as they approached an arched bridge.

"What's up Harry? We should do this one alright with just an inch to spare according to your notes." Arthur shaded his eyes against the sun's glare as he looked at the arch of the bridge and the height restriction marked on its brickwork. The diesel ticked over unevenly as they both looked at the bridge; luckily they were on a quiet road so there was no traffic behind them.

"I am not sure about this one Arthur – it just doesn't look right to me. I'm getting out to have a look – you bring her on slowly." Harry climbed down from the cab and walked over to the bridge; he looked up and down and then walked across to the side of the stone wall of the bridge to check where the road surface met the wall. "Arthur – come and have a look at this!" Arthur got down from the cab. "Look, they have just put fresh Tarmac down; it will have reduced the height clearance! I think we've had it here – we'll have to find another way."

"Even if we can, it is going to take hours…… let's give it a try."

"All right, but I don't think she'll go" Harry shook his head. Arthur climbed back up into the cab and revving the engine he inched slowly forwards, lining up for the centre of the road. Harry climbed up onto 1462's buffer beam, as the arch came closer.

"Stop!" Yelled Harry. "Come and have a look, I guess about an inch too low."

Arthur climbed up alongside Harry.

"I don't ruddy believe it – just an inch!"

"We could cut the top off the stack." Suggested Harry.

"Come off it – that would ruin her." Arthur replied, hurt at the thought of such an act of vandalism.

"We had better think of something quick then, we are blocking the road and someone is bound to be coming along soon." Harry couldn't think of any other solution. A group of young boys had come under the bridge on their bikes, and had stopped to watch the proceedings. "Push off!" Harry shouted.

His remark caused riotous laughter from the boys. "You push off yourself Mister – but you can't though, can you?" A boy called Sandy answered back.

"Ruddy kids." Muttered Harry.

"How much have you got to cut off the top then?" asked Sandy, the only one really interested in their predicament?

"About an inch." Arthur answered.

Sandy propped his bike against the side of the bridge, and slowly walked around the front of the vehicle, he stopped and kicked the off side front tyre. Harry and Arthur watched.

"We had this at school the other day." he said, going back for his bike.

"You had what at school?" called Harry trying to sound friendly.

"This!" Sandy said.

"What?" Harry's voice was getting a little louder.

"A lorry or something going under a low bridge."

"At school?" Harry and Arthur asked together.

"Yep – and we worked out the answer." Sandy grinned up at them.

"What was the answer?" asked Harry, trying to keep from climbing down and giving the boy a clip around the ear hole.

"Ah, that's for us to know and you to find out." again he grinned up at them. "We might tell you if you paid us."

"What?" Growled Harry "I'll come down there…….."

"Hang on Harry, he might be on to something and we are well and truly stuck" Arthur muttered, "All right sunshine – how much?"

Sandy thought for a moment. "Two bob each," he nodded his head towards his companions, who nodded back.

"What?" Said Harry, "There are five of you, that's ten shillings!"

"You're quick you are Mister, and no mistake!" Sandy grinned up at them.

"Why you little Monkey. I'll ….." Harry spluttered.

"How do we know you have the answer? You could be trying it on." Arthur cut in.

"Look, Mister I am not going to give you any clues, right? What we know will work but it's up to you, and you'd better hurry up 'cause we have to be going home." Sandy put his right leg over his cross bar ready to push off.

"Wait!" Called Arthur. "Look Harry, we have to give in. I'm not going to cut that chimney and we haven't got any ideas of our own – let's give them ten bob and give it a chance."

"All right." Harry climbed down and went across to Sandy. He fished into his trouser pocket and pulled out four half crowns, he opened his fist to show Sandy, and clinked the coins together.

"Ain't you got five two bobs mister?" Sandy scowled.

"No" said Harry, slowly moving his left hand and grasping the handlebar of Sandy's bike " – just in case you're trying to pull a fast one." With his other hand he passed over the four half crowns to Sandy, who gripped them tightly.

"Now, what do we do?" Harry said the words slowly and deliberately.

"Let some air out of your tyres – it works, honest."

"What did he say?" Called Arthur.

"He says to let some air out of the tyres". Harry shouted back.

"Why didn't we think of that? The kid's right!" Arthur was grinning.

Sandy's handle bars stayed gripped.

"Let us go Mister, we told you what to do!" Sandy shook the bike backwards and forwards.

"It's alright Harry let him go – thanks kids, that's one I won't forget!" Arthur waved at Sandy and the other boys. Released, Sandy rode away with his right hand clutching the money raised triumphal into the air, the rest of the boys cheering behind him.

"That has just cost me ten bob." Said Harry as Arthur came down.

"Never mind that, look he's right – we can let them down quite a bit, that will drop us more than an inch, we get under the arch and then we blow them up again with the compressor on the wagon." Arthur looked at Harry.

"You never told me there was a compressor!" Harry raised his eyebrows in exasperation.

"I can't remember to tell you everything! Look, you go to the other side and see if you can see a place to pull off the road to inflate them again so we don't block the road."

Harry ran under the bridge to the far side and waved at Arthur, indicating a piece of open ground on the other side of the arch. Arthur went round all the wheels of the transporter dropping the pressure of each carefully to keep enough air inside so as not to damage the tyre walls while still dropping the ride height.

Harry meanwhile was up on the buffer beam watching the rim of 1462s chimney slowly drop under the arch. "That's it Arthur – she should go now." Harry shouted down. Revving the engine and feathering the clutch, Arthur moved the transporter and 1462 slowly under the bridge praying all the time that the Tarmac used in the repair was level.

"Nice one! Keep her going Arthur – she's going to make it!" Harry studied the underside of the bridge and breathed a sigh of relief as they came out on to the other side; soon they were moving very slowly off the road and onto the space next to it.

A car beeped as it came under the bridge behind them; the lady occupant shook her fist up at Harry. "I have been waiting nearly five minutes behind you – shouldn't that engine be on a track?"

"Sorry Missus!" replied Harry "we had a lot of err, punctures."

Arthur pulled out the air hose and showed Harry how to connect it to the tyre valves. He climbed back into the cab to switch over the gear to drive the compressor and they were in business, it took nearly half an hour to re-inflate all the wheels and check the pressures.

"What if we come across any more bridges like that?" Harry asked.

"Just let's hope we don't mate, 'cause we'll never get to your place on time if we do!" Crunching into bottom gear they pulled back onto the road again, an hour had passed and they were making good progress. "There's a transport café up this road, we can pull in for a bite to eat – what do you say Harry?"

"Fine by me."

"And a good cup of tea." Harry grinned. "Look there it is, up on the left past those trees – just what the doctor ordered!"

Arthur went down through the gear box bringing their speed down, but he did not notice the deep ruts in the hard packed earth as he drew into the truck park, the transporter bucked up and down violently as they came to a halt. "Sorry Harry old mate, you OK? I hope everything is alright, one more bump like that and we could have lost old 1462." Arthur was worried about the vehicle. They checked the transporter over, but everything looked fine and they had not burst any tyres, so they went into the café for their tea.

Their hunger satisfied they came out of the café, Arthur checked his watch. "Nearly five, we should be at your place in a couple of hours."

"I'll sure be glad when we are Arthur." Harry stretched his arms above his head.

"Let's have you then Harry boy." Arthur swung up to the cab, and settled in his seat.

"Good girl" he said as the engine roared into life, with first gear selected he let the clutch out and they moved gently forward, but suddenly there was a loud bang and they stopped.

They looked at each other. "Oh, Hell." They both jumped out of the cab, Arthur hurriedly checked around the wheels – what could it be?

He frantically looked for any tell tale signs, oil dripping, anything hanging off – nothing!

"What could have caused that bang? You know Arthur, the only other time I heard a wagon make a sound like that was when I was in the army, when our truck broke its half shafts."

"You could be right Harry, to tell you the truth I did not want to think that."

"What we going to do now?"

"You watch the drive wheels, let's try it again." More in hope than expectation Arthur climbed into the cab and started up the engine again. "Here we go Harry!" slowly the accelerator went down and the clutch came out, but no joy – a grinding noise and no movement. Arthur turned the engine off. "We have had it, we cannot move another inch!" Arthur banged both hands down onto the steering wheel in frustration.

"I can't give in now, the others will think I have done this deliberately – we have got to do something." Harry was pacing up and down. "How much time have we got?"

"What do you mean Harry? – how much time…" Arthur leant dejectedly against a road wheel.

"I have got to phone Titfield – what time is it again?"

"Just on five" replied Arthur.

"We could just do it, but we have got to start now." Harry was looking round for a phone. "There!" he cried excitedly, "There by the café – quick Arthur, give me your change."

Arthur dug out every coin in his pocket and gave them to Harry. As Harry was running to the phone box, he shouted back to Arthur. "How many miles to go?"

"Forty five miles." Was the answer he got back. Harry pulled open the phone box door, pulled out a piece of paper with his Titfield numbers, and slammed all the coins down on the coin box.

"I'll try Dickey first!" his hands were shaking as he dialed for the operator, "Hallo, Yeah, Titfield 412 please."

"That will be one shilling please," came the operator's plummy voice.

"A shilling croaked Harry."

"It is not six o'clock yet caller." Said the voice.

"OK, OK, hang on." Harry sorted through his money, and dropped two sixpences into the call box.

"Trying to connect you." The plummy voice said.

Ring Ring…. Ring Ring…. It seemed ages to Harry before the call was finally picked up, Harry pressed button A. "Hallo! Hallo! Is Dickey there?"

"Err no, not at the moment, who's calling?"

"It's me – Harry Hawkins. Listen I have not got much time, can you take this number down?"

"Hallo Harry, have not heard from you in a while, hang on, right I've got a pencil – go ahead."

"I'm on Foreham 173, it's a phone box. Get Dickey to phone here as soon as possible and tell him not to dowse his fire – I am going to need him and his loco straight away."

"He should be here soon Harry; I will get him to ring you soon as he comes in."

"Has he been working with Fossy or Bomb lately?"

"I think so Harry, I…." The pips started, peep, peep, peep, indicating that the phone was about to disconnect.

"Don't forget!" shouted Harry, but the money had run out. He tried Fossy next, but got no answer and pressed button B to get his money back.

Bomb was next, the plummy operator got the number, and after a couple of rings Bomb answered. Harry hit button A "Bomb, it's Harry, is your engine alright? Is it fired up?"

"Harry boy, how're you doing? Yeh, it's still in steam, I've only just got in – she's outside."

"Look Bomb, I need your help, and Dickey's, and Fossey's. I'm at Foreham, it's about Forty five miles from you and I need a tow."

"Blimey Harry! Forty five miles – hang on though, you don't need three of us to tow your roller."

"I haven't got my roller, it's a low loader with a steam engine on it, we are looking at a hundred tons at least!" Silence.

"Bomb, are you there? Look Bomb I have not got much time, I need you and the other two here at Fordham Transport café on the Ridgely road just as soon as possible."

"Righto Harry, but it's going to take a few hours to get to you – what if the other two are cold?"

"Then you tow them until they have steam up too, come on Bomb I am desperate."

"Fair dos Harry, I know where you are – we'll see you as soon as we can." The pips went again and Harry put the phone down, Arthur was waiting outside.

"That's it; I will wait until after six before I phone the Vicar and the Squire, I only hope they don't think I did this on purpose."

"What you talking about? It didn't have anything to do with you – I snapped those half shafts. Come on; let's get another cup of tea." Harry's throat was dry, so he nodded and followed Arthur back into the café.

Six o'clock and Harry called the Reverend Weech from the phone box to tell him the news and his plans to get 1462 to Titfield.

"I am sure it will work Harry, you have to have faith, now what do you want us to do?"

"See if you can get Mallingford shed to have the carriage ready for collection on the Titfield side of the sidings, we won't have time to stand around – and try to get Mr Blakeworth to delay the Ministry bloke."

"Right Harry. Look, give me your number in case anything crops up at our end." Harry gave him the number.

"Now we have to wait." Harry said pushing open the phone box door and looking at Arthur waiting outside. The phone rang behind him; he turned around and picked it up.

"Are you ever going to get off that ruddy phone?" It was Dickey Birds voice.

"Dickey – good lad, what's happening?"

"Fossey's loco is cold, but he is getting her fired. Mine is ready, and so is Bomb's and the wives are making us sandwiches. I'm going to Fossey's and I will tow him till he's got pressure up, so we should all see you in about three hours time."

"Good on you Dickey, I'll never forget this. You are real pals – have you and Fossey still got your cranes?"

"Yeh and they are working, see you soon old mate – so long."

Harry turned again to Arthur "It is good to have real mates."

"You are right Harry my old son, now let's get a bit of kip – we are going to need it." They both climbed back up in to the cab and put their feet up on the dashboard to make themselves more comfortable.

"Arthur how did you come by your place then?" Asked Harry, not really ready for sleep.

"I got it from my Dad. It's a grand old place, and the ivy covering the front always looks good – you really did not see much of it, I've got about fifty acres all told." Arthur was very proud of his birthplace.

"That's handy getting it off your Dad."

"Yes, trouble is I had plans to buy some withdrawn steam engines and put a track down to run them on but, they would not give me planning permission. I have liked engines since my Army days at Longmoor."

"Longmoor, then you must have been in the Royal Engineers, the same as me?"

"You are right Harry, they taught me how to fire and drive, and I knew when I got out I would want to have engines of my own."

"Cor, same as me, I went on to rollers, took to them straight away I did, worked with nothing else since I got out."

"Ah, but you're lucky Harry, I had to find the money, but I have been lucky too, bought the Transporter cheap at an Army sale and got old 1462 at virtually scrap price."

"If you don't mind me asking Arthur, how did you manage it?"

"Mushrooms Harry."

"Mushrooms? You've got to be across the fields early in the morning to get mushrooms haven't you? And that's if you know where to look for 'em."

"I told you I have been lucky. I was in the mob with a feller who used to be a Chef, and he was always going on as how he could never get enough mushrooms for his Restaurant, and if he did get any they were always expensive, because he was in London."

"You're right Arthur; I don't suppose there are many fields in London."

"Well I done a bit of reading up about mushrooms, and I reckoned that after the War I could supply him with all the mushrooms he needed, and at a good price."

"But how?" Harry was shaking his head.

"Out the back of my place I've got lots of old buildings, the old man were always going to knock them down. Anyway when I got out, I buy some spores, fill the old places full of compost, kept everything dark and in no time at all I had a crop. Now I supply a lot of London's restaurants – I've made plenty of money Harry, more than enough for me and my hobby."

"Blimey, that's a tale and no mistake." Harry was scratching his head.

"When I heard your place needed an engine I thought to myself great, 1462 could get a good run there and Titfield isn't that far away. I am hoping to do a deal so any more engines I buy I can run on your lines, so you see it's good for me and it's good for Titfield!"

"Cor!" said Harry, his eye lids started to droop and they both started to drop off to sleep.

The three road locos were now on their way, Fossy had got steam up on his engine and they were travelling at a good fifteen miles an hour. Three powerful Fowler B6s with short canopies, rolling in line across the evening countryside. They were quite a sight trundling along and local children from the villages they passed through ran alongside.

It was after nine o'clock when they finally sounded their whistles to announce their arrival at the transport café at Foreham. After drawing up outside, they went into the café for a cup of tea and to plan the tow back to Titfield.

Arthur looked at his new companions. First Bomb, a big man, well over six foot tall, a shock of unruly blond hair with sideburns growing down in line with his mouth, sun tanned and with a round pleasant face and a broad Devon accent. Fossey, like Bomb in his early forties, but slim and about five eight in height, sharp featured, dark short cropped hair, and also from Devon. Dickey was maybe a little overweight, kept that way by a regular intake of strong ale, but always happy, with rosy cheeks and about the same height as Bomb. They all had deep blue eyes.

"Have you got brakes Arthur?" Fossey wanted to know.

"If I run the engine I will have air for the brakes."

"Good, then we don't need a trace loco." Fossey said.

"What do you mean?" Asked Arthur.

"Well it means we don't have to put a loco behind your transporter to act as a brake, which means we will make better time." Harry nodded and the loco men nodded back.

Tea drank they went outside, Dickey, Fossey, and then Bomb lined up their locomotives and fixed solid tow bars between each of them in turn and then on to Arthur's truck.

The sky had changed to that dusky very dark blue and the stars were just appearing. With three toots, and a blast from Arthur's horn they started on their way, they were going to have to keep to a steady five miles an hour if they were going to get to Titfield on time.

As three individual engines on their outward journey they had made a fair noise as they moved along, but now that they were linked together and towing seventy odd tons, the noise they made was deafening and the ground shook as they passed.

Villages and hamlets were shaken awake as they rumbled slowly past, false teeth rattled in their water filled glasses on bedside tables, milk bottles clinked together on door steps, dozing dogs ran from front gates, whilst fierce cats skulked underneath hedgerows, cowering from the strange steaming beasts. In fields along their way cows got up and ran away from the road to get away from the din of the fire breathing monsters.

Though they needed every moment, they still had to stop periodically to oil their moving parts and to de-clinker their fires as they had done on their journey from Titfield. The air was warm and scented; it was a lovely balmy summer's night, a night when they all felt it was good to be alive. One obstacle was waiting for them though, about an hour from home they would come to the Old Barracks Bank, a gradient that lasted for three miles and which climbed in parts as steeply as one in ten, they all knew this would be their greatest test!

At eleven o'clock that same night Mr Valentine, having supped and dined well, left the Function rooms in Mallingford. He waved goodbye to the doorman, took in a deep breath of air, put his Trilby hat on the back of his head and turned in the direction of Mallingford station. He was on his way to get his taxi – but on the way he would call in to his second favourite watering hole in the town, the Buffet on the platform of Mallingford Station…

Usually, whilst their train was halted at Mallingford, he would slip away and leave Joan and his own buffet coach for half an hour or so in order to meet his other platonic paramour – Mrs Ely in the station buffet. Mrs Ely was a fine figure of a woman, smartly dressed, her dyed blond hair was piled high on top of her head and her movements were precise and feminine. She dispensed her wares with delicate movements of her slim fingers with crimson painted nails and returned Mr Valentine's admiration from her domain behind the solid Mahogany counter of the buffet. With its glass shelves, optics and ornate glass cases displaying sandwiches and other culinary delights, the room had not changed since the Nineteen Thirties. It was a time capsule from Mr Valentine's lost youth and he loved both its ambiance and its occupant.

"Mr Valentine!" Mrs Ely announced at his arrival, adjusting her hair for maximum effect and polishing a fresh glass in anticipation, her reaction left the other occupants of the buffet in no doubt as to Mr Valentine's status.

"Mrs Ely – my good lady! Please, my usual, and do have one for your good self." Mr Valentine raised his hat and moved it to his chest, reaching the counter he dropped the hat onto it in his customary manner.

"That Larry the taxi driver was in earlier, said that he had a customer, but would be back for your good self later." She looked steadily into Mr Valentine's eyes as she placed his Gin and Tonic before him, her makeup maybe a little over done.

"Thank you dear lady – your very good health! Bit quiet tonight eh?"

"It is Mr Valentine, no more trains to come in now and just the Newcastle out before midnight. I've got time to clean all my glasses ready for the girls in the morning." Mrs Ely used the term Girls loosely; neither she nor any of her staff would be seeing fifty again.

"I was just admiring your lovely floor Mrs Ely, those beautiful Black and White tiles really do stand out now you've polished them, and all those years old and they still look quite magnificent."

Before she could answer, the door from the platform swung open and an attractive young woman with natural blonde hair and wearing a smart Camel coat entered. She smiled at Mrs Ely and Mr Valentine. "Good evening, has the Newcastle train gone yet?"

"Oh no dear lady, not for a while yet – please won't you join us, let me buy you a small drink while you wait."

The young woman looked at Mr Valentine uncertainly, not quite sure what to say, Mrs Ely cut in. "Oh, Mr Valentine is gentleman beyond reproach my dear, do not be afraid."

The young lady smiled and moved to the counter.

"Thank you Mr Valentine, that would be very nice, perhaps a Gin and Tonic?"

"Mrs Ely dear would you do the honours? I must just excuse myself – a call of nature don't you know." Mr Valentine turned away and went to the door.

While Mrs Ely was cutting a slice of lemon to put in the drink, the young woman quickly dropped a little white pill into Mr Valentine's glass and swirled the drink around to dissolve it. This act was completed before Mrs Ely had turned back to the counter.

"There you are my dear, a fine gentleman is our Mr Valentine, and he has been coming in here for all of twenty years."

The young lady smiled and sipped her drink, Mr Valentine returned and all three continued to chat, until the young lady looked at her watch. "Oh, it must be time for my train now" she finished her drink, "thanks you very much for your hospitality Mr Valentine."

"A pleasure my dear, a pleasure. Look it's about time I made a move myself, allow me to accompany you to your train. Good night Mrs Ely and I'll see you tomorrow – our new engine should be running."

"Good night Mr Valentine – and good luck for tomorrow!" Mrs Ely washed the glasses and looking at the clock saw it would soon be closing time.

They walked slowly along the platform towards the waiting train. "What was that about an engine Mr Valentine?" The young woman linked into his arm.

"Oh, I and some friends own our own branch line to Titfield and we have had a little spot bother of late, but it will be all sorted out tomorrow." Mr Valentine had suddenly started to feel very tired. "My goodness I think today has taken more out of me than I realized, I think I need to sit down."

"Look we are at the train now, why don't you come into my compartment; it doesn't go for another ten minutes and it'll be more comfortable than the platform bench." He followed her on to the train and sat down heavily into a corner seat, of the compartment.

"There you are that's better – why don't you close your eyes for a few minutes? I'll be sure to let you know before the train goes." Mr Valentine eyelids dropped, they were suddenly becoming heavier and her soothing voice trailed further into the distance, soon he was dead to the World as he fell into a deep drug induced sleep.

The young woman quietly left the compartment and stood on the platform looking in on him. There was a shrill blast of the whistle as the train started off, but it did not disturb Mr Valentine and the Newcastle train left the station with Mr Valentine on board, oblivious to all around him.

Three men moved out of the shadows and stood beside her. "Well done my dear." Alistair said "He's on his way now!" he handed the girl a five pound note.

"It seems a bit of a mean trick, sending him all that way – he never mentioned he was going to get married once, seems a bit odd if you ask me."

"Look don't worry, I'm his best man. He is going to marry our Mum but he doesn't get hitched for a couple of days and there's family up there to meet him – so what's the harm?" He added "He would have smelled a rat straight away if he had seen us!"

She put the five pound note in her bag and walked off; it was her first acting job.

"Goodbye Mr Valentine." Alistair chuckled to himself "Time to make a couple of phone calls…" A quiet street and a phone box away from the station were needed and the three men soon found one. Alistair dialled the number on the piece of paper he produced from his pocket.

"Keep ringing until I get there…" muttered Reverend Weech as he made his way down the stairs to his study, where the phone was. "Hallo, Titfield Vicarage!" He spoke into the handset – a phone box he thought, hearing the click of a button. "It must be Harry, hallo…. hallo… Harry – what's the matter?"

"What's the matter Reverend? I will tell you – Mr Valentine, that's what the matter is. We have him and if you don't phone the Ministry and say you are closing your railway down, then you won't see him again…"

"What? Oh my goodness, you don't mean, you cannot – poor Mr Valentine!" The Reverend Weech did not know which way to turn.

"You just phone the Ministry first thing in the morning – or else no more MrValentine." Alistair put the black handset back onto the cradle. "Why didn't we think of that before? We must be getting soft." he laughed, nastily.

Reverend Weech sat down on the stairs by the phone, his mind in turmoil. "Gordon, I must phone Gordon!" He dialled through the operator; it took a while before Gordon answered.

"Sam! Sam – calm down! What's happened?"

"It's Mr Valentine – he's been kidnapped."

"What?" Said Gordon in disbelief.

"It's true, they phoned to say if we want to see Walter again we must phone the Ministry first thing and tell them we are closing down the railway."

"Did you recognize the voice Sam? Think – it's important!"

"I don't know Gordon, I really don't know, and what are we going to do? I am sure they mean it and I could not put Mr Valentine's life in danger, not even for our railway."

"Steady Sam, it might not come to that, it might be a hoax. Before we do anything else you phone Mrs Valentine, but try not to alarm her. I will phone Mr Blakeworth."

They made their phone calls and Gordon got back to the Reverend Weech. "Mr Blakeworth agrees with me Sam, it might be a hoax, but obviously we cannot take any chances, what did Mrs Valentine say?"

"He's not there, he was in Mallingford at a function, and should have been home before now, so I told her he could be at Dan's place."

"Look Sam, Harry is moving heaven and earth to get that engine here. I don't want to give up now so we'll sit it out, and if you think you have to phone the Ministry then wait until nine o'clock in the morning." It was agreed and they both put their phones down and went back to bed for a night of fitful sleep.

They were parked up on a quiet stretch of road, the sky was inky black and the night was still warm. The three enginemen and Harry were standing by the lead loco. All that could be heard was the steam easing from the boilers, and distant barking of foxes. They had used a nearby stream to re-fill their tanks and now after another round of oiling up they could relax for a few minutes. "Tea up." Arthur appeared carrying five mugs of tea. "Doing alright I reckon, eh but it's a nice night – look at those stars, never seen them like that before."

"I'll just be glad when we get there," replied Harry, sipping his tea. The others all nodded in agreement. Tea finished they mounted their engines for the next spell, after a starting toot from the lead engine they set off rumbling on into what was left of the night. Harry looked at his watch, the dawn had broken a little while back and things were going well, but it was six o'clock already and they still had fifteen miles to go. Soon they would be at the Old Barracks Bank, they rumbled on while sleepy eyed householders along their route looked out of their bedroom windows to see what had woken them up.

The fire laid in 1462's box was building up nicely; Harry had lit up at their last tea stop so that the new engine would be ready to go as soon as they got to the railway. After another hour on the road, they pulled over to oil up and clean their locomotive's fires – ahead lay the Old Barracks bank. A stream ran by the road here, so once again they ran the water lines out to fill their tanks – this would be their last opportunity to fill them before Titfield.

"Everyone ready?" Dick called, the others waved in acknowledgement and Arthur tapped his horn, opening their locomotives up and with pistons flying, they headed towards the bank, hoping to get a good speed up before hitting it

CHAPTER 14

Tuesday

—

Inspection day II

Mr Valentine stirred; he opened his eyes and blinked in the morning light. It took a couple of seconds for his eyes to focus and he looked around the compartment in bewilderment. Had he celebrated too well last night? Had the new carriage arrived and was he in it… then he heard seagulls. Seagulls? They never flew this far inland – his head ached.

"Newcastle! Newcastle! All change, all change…" the compartment door drew open. "Newcastle sir, can I see your ticket please? I didn't want to disturb you last night."

The burly guard stood in the doorway with his hand out.

"Err, ticket?" Murmured Mr Valentine.

"That's right Sir, ticket."

Mr Valentine tried to gather his wits. "Newcastle, you say, how did I get on a train to Newcastle when all I wanted was a taxi?"

"All I know sir is that you are on this train and this is Newcastle, now have you got a ticket?"

"Err, no." said Mr Valentine, his mouth now very dry.

"Right then, let's be having you, the Transport Police can take care of you." The guard lifted Mr Valentine from his seat and bundled him off the train and along to the Police office. "Sit there." The guard dropped him into an old high backed chair – Mr Valentine put his head in his hands and groaned. "No ticket, and he got on at Mallingford Junction – you sort him out." he swept out of the door and back to his train.

The balding Sergeant sat opposite Mr Valentine looking him over, he was obviously not a vagrant, being very well dressed and with expensive clothes. "Now then Sir, how did you come to not have a ticket for your journey?" he asked.

"I really don't know Sergeant, one minute I was talking to Mrs Ely in the buffet, and then I woke up here – I think I can remember a young lady."

"A young lady eh? Now then Sir what would your wife say?"

"Oh, my wife!" gasped Mr Valentine "She will be worried – I've never stayed out all night before, I've stayed out late, but never all night…… well maybe just the once." He groaned again.

"Right then Sir, first things first, have you got the price of a ticket?" "Of course," answered Mr Valentine, and pulled his wallet out, and put it on the desk.

"Well that's one problem solved. Now what do you want to do?"

"I must phone my wife, and my friends – it is a very important day today."

The Sergeant put the phone in front of Mr Valentine. "Help yourself."

"Walter – where are you?" came Felicity's angry voice in the earpiece.

"I am in Newcastle my dear, please don't ask me how or why because I don't know myself – how is everything going at your end?"

"Reverend Weech was on the telephone after midnight asking for you, he said you were with Dan – is he in Newcastle too?"

"No Felicity, he is not. Look my dear I must phone the Padre, what time do you have?"

"It is nearly nine o'clock."

"Right, got to go dear, goodbye." He put the receiver down and dialled another number.

Harry watched the engines from the buffer beam of 1462, they were doing well but the Barracks Bank had taken its toll, and they were now down to a walking pace. Another quarter of a mile and they would be at the summit but they were now slowing down, imperceptibly but steadily – you could count the revolutions of the big back wheels and Harry was worried that they were going to stall before reaching the top of the bank.

Harry shouted above the din. "Right! Nearly there lads, give your engines full gear when I say – you'll be able to recover your fires once we are over the top." They all heard him and raised their arms in acknowledgment. Harry waited until the gradient tightened into the final ascent and gave the signal. "Right, give it all you've got – Now!"

As the locomotives were put into full gear the dawn sky was darkened by three columns of cinder laden smoke blasting upwards and the resulting turn of power took the procession surging forwards and after a few more

minutes of deafening blast the first loco reached the summit, with the other two and 1462 followed steadily behind. Having made it, they eased back their regulators and gave their iron mounts all of their concentration as they gathered speed on the other side of the hill, all the time getting closer to Titfield.

Harry waved his hat in the air – with a bit of luck they would get to the crossing by nine o'clock!

Reverend Weech looked at the mantle clock and then checked his pocket watch. "It is nine o'clock Gordon, I had better phone now."

"Leave it just a little longer Sam – you never know."

"How can we wait any longer Gordon, when our friend could be in mortal danger? He reached for the handset just as it began to ring. "Hallo."

"Hallo, Mr Weech is that you?"

"It's Mr Valentine!" cried Sam. "Walter, are you safe?"

"Safe? Safe? Of course I'm safe!" He turned to the Sergeant, "I think the pressure is getting to him, he's asking me if I am safe!"

"Walter!" called Sam.

"I am fine Sam, I'm in Newcastle, no…don't ask me how I got here – I will tell you all about it when I see you. How is Harry doing?"

"We are hoping he will be at the crossing about now, we must get down to the station – when will you be back?"

Mr.Valentine looked at the Sergeant. "There is a train heading south in a couple of minutes, so you had better buy a ticket…" The sergeant grinned at Mr Valentine and handed him back his wallet.

"Got to go Sam – see you later!" he put the phone down.

"I need two tickets!" he said to the Sergeant, and they both hurried along the platform to the ticket office.

They positioned the transporter carefully over the level crossing with its centre lined up along the track, Fossy, Bomb and Dickey then drove their engines to one side and after parking they went to help Arthur disengage the rear wheels of the trailer. Once this was done they used the sleepers and spare rails that Arthur had packed on to the trailer and built a ramp that would allow 1462 to be gently winched off the trailer and on to the track.

Arthur slowly let 1462 roll backwards off the trailer and on to the ramp by carefully controlling the winch, while Harry stood on the footplate ready to operate the brake. After inching down the ramp, first her trailing wheels and then both sets of driving wheels dropped down on to the railway line, Harry applied the brake and 1462 was safely standing on the Titfield branch line.

After checking around the locomotive Harry opened the regulator and set 1462 back a few yards towards Titfield in order to clear the level crossing. Jumping down from the footplate he helped the others dismantle the ramp, and then once the trailer was clear they jacked the ramp up and refitted the rear wheels to the trailer. Fossy then climbed aboard his engine and after moving carefully into position he towed Arthur's transporter and its trailer away from the track and on to a good area of land nearby that belonged to the railway. Arthur looked at it thoughtfully; this would be a good place for some extra sidings or even a shed – just the place to house a private collection of rolling stock.

His thoughts were interrupted by Harry, "Right lads I am off to Mallingford to pick up the carriage, take your engines up to the station and pass the word to Reverend Weech and the Squire that we are running a little late, but that we should be back on time." He looked down from the footplate "You want to fire for me Arthur?"

"Right with you Harry!" Arthur ran across and climbed aboard.

Harry opened the regulator and 1462 emitted a deep bark as she moved off and steamed off through the level crossing and on towards Mallingford. "Let's see what she can do Arthur, we need to be at Mallingford Sidings just as soon as possible. So saying he opened the regulator and wound the locomotive towards mid gear and soon the trees and hedges were rushing by as they steamed along the branch line at a speed considerably in excess of the 25mph laid down by their light railway order. Arthur was enjoying himself being on a footplate again, all the trouble of the last twenty four hours had been worth it.

The Reverend had booked their locomotive into the sidings at Mallingford for nine o'clock; Harry was hoping there would be no delay in getting into the sidings to get the carriage. As they came to the sidings signal box, one of the signalmen was standing on the walkway outside the box; he waved and pointed to his right. There, standing on the first siding in the yard was the LNER carriage, resplendent in its teak livery it sparkled in the morning sunlight.

"Eh but you must have friends in high places" said the signalman, "the yard cleaners gave that a good going over last night – inside and out!"

"Thanks!" called Harry, and once the siding signal was pulled off he moved 1462 across the points and on to the first siding, easing up to the coach until the buffers touched. Arthur dropped down to the track, moving to the front of the 1462 he swung the coupling up on to the locomotive's hook and screwed the link up tight before connecting the brake hoses. "Let's take them home Arthur" Harry grinned, and after checking the brake vacuum he gently opened the regulator and eased their new train out of the sidings and towards Titfield.

The three road engines all whistled as they rolled into Titfield station yard, where a crowd of well wishers had already gathered. Reverend Weech and the Squire walked across to them to shake their hands. "Well done! Well done indeed! You are all most splendid fellows, how can we ever thank you?" Fossy, Bomb and Dickey smiled down from their engines and pleasantries were exchanged.

"But what's happening – has Harry gone to Mallingford already? Time is getting on." The Reverend Weech consulted his pocket watch for the umpteenth time.

"He should be on his way by now Vicar, if you will pardon the expression he was going like a bat out of hell when he left us." Dickey smiled.

"Twenty five minutes to go – now have we thought of everything?" Reverend Weech looked at the Squire.

"The guard's van is just beyond the crossing, the Bedford is out of the way on the siding, so all that Harry has to do when he turns up is to uncouple, run around the carriage and then shunt back to pick up the guard's van and couple up."

"Where's that Ministry feller?" chipped in Dan, "haven't seen him about yet."

"He's with Mr Blakeworth, they will be coming up from the Manor, and very soon if I'm not mistaken." the Reverend checked his watch yet again.

"Don't worry Sam, he won't be here until ten o'clock on the dot and we still have ten minutes," Gordon took a nervous look at his own watch as he finished speaking.

They all looked up as they heard a train whistle and within a few minutes they saw 1462 approaching them in reverse, with a beautiful teak carriage in tow and Harry waving to them from the locomotive's footplate. Joan was jumping up and down, and waving back. "Oh Reverend – don't they look magnificent!"

They walked on to the platform just as 1462 and its train drew to a halt. "My, my, she does look splendid – well done both of you! Now Harry, we only have a few moments to get her ready, we need to run around and…"

Harry cut in. "Don't you worry Mr Weech – Arthur and me are getting to be expert at this game, we'll have this lot sorted out in no time at all." Arthur jumped down to uncouple, stood aside and Harry ran forwards before running around and then shunting the new train together for the very first time.

At exactly ten o'clock, Mr Blakeworth, Mr Clegg, and Mr Ruddock walked up the small lane to the station. The new locomotive, the sparkling teak carriage and Gordon's van all stood proudly on the track alongside the platform, ready for their passengers. As the party walked over the level crossing, looking to their left the Ministry men caught sight of *Thunderbolt* back at the shed. "Your best stock then today, I takes it Mr Blakeworth?" Asked Mr Clegg.

"No, this is normal stock Sir. Contrary to what you might have heard *Thunderbolt* was only ever going to be a temporary measure."

Mr Ruddock stopped, and tapping Mr.Clegg on the arm indicated over to the siding, he had caught sight of the OB Bedford standing next to the steam crane. Mr Ruddock stopped and took in the bus, with its rail wheels still bolted to its hubs. He looked questioningly at Mr Blakeworth… "A little experiment." Mr Blakeworth answered with a slight smile. Mr Ruddock smiled back while his colleague shook his head in disbelief; they walked on and up onto the platform and Gordon opened the carriage door.

"Hmm, LNER – it's a long way from home." Mr Clegg looked at Gordon enquiringly.

"Its home now Mr Clegg – we only use the best rolling stock."

"Humph!" exclaimed Mr Clegg entering the carriage.

Mr Ruddock smiled at Gordon as he followed his colleague inside. "Well done." he said quietly.

"A bar, I see." Mr Clegg looked round at the quite opulent carriage.

The Squire appeared at the door. "This is a particularly fine carriage, not only do we have a bar counter, there is a small kitchen, a toilet, and as you can see substantial twin and single seating with tables." He smiled at the inspector.

"Which way would you like to sit, forwards or backwards?" Joan pulled two seats back from one of the tables.

"This is really quite smart" said Mr Ruddock. "I always admired the LNER restaurant cars and this was just third class – quite remarkable." he made himself comfortable in a seat facing the engine, Mr Clegg choosing the seat opposite him. Most of the well wishers came on board too; it was to be no private trip today!

"It's time we were off Gordon – good luck to us all!" said Reverend Weech, and so saying he strode towards the cab of 1462.

"I'll ride up on the bunker Reverend" said Harry "and Arthur is going in the van with the Squire." Dan was already on the footplate attending to the fire, Harry clambered upon to the coal and the Reverend checked the various gauges ready for departure.

Gordon blew the whistle and waved his flag, and they were off.

"Oh Dan, It's like old times," said Reverend Weech, patting Dan's shoulder.

Harry peered through from the bunker "I never saw Mr Valentine – Reverend?" he inquired.

"He's at Newcastle Harry." said the Reverend in a matter of fact way, as if he went there every day.

"Oh." said Harry, and even in his uncomfortable position and with the noise from 1462 he was so tired that he was soon fast asleep amongst the coals.

The Pearce brothers had watched the road engines heading for the station and they had seen Harry and 1462 heading back to Titfield with the new carriage, they knew now that all their scheming had come to nothing. "What now?" Asked Fergal, "any more bright ideas?"

"Wait a minute," said Alistair. "They brought that engine back on a transporter, where is it? The lanes around here are too narrow to park it on, so where is it?"

"The only place big enough for that is at the crossing," answered Fraser. "Come on – it's only down this lane!" They ran down the lane and around the bend, they saw the transporter. "Quick we'll block the line with it!" shouted Fraser.

"But if we block the line that will prove to those Ministry blokes that their troubles weren't their fault – no we'll try something at the water tower." They ran up the line towards Titfield, out of breath they made it to the water tower before the train carrying the inspectors had reached it.

"Right, listen. Fergal and Fraser – you go down the bank behind the tower, and shout help just as they finish taking on water. When they go looking for you, I'll nip up to the loco and let the brakes off, alright?" The two nodded, and moved down the bank; Alistair had only just got himself hidden in the undergrowth as the train came into sight.

"Right you are Dan; we had better take on a little water." The Reverend climbed down to work the chain as Dan opened the tank flap.

"She'll do Reverend!" called Dan as the water spilled over.

"Help! Help! Down here – we are hurt!" came the cries.

"Quickly Dan, come quickly, there's someone in distress down here." Reverend Weech was starting down the bank.

"Hang on now Vicar, it could be funny business" Dan swung down from the engine.

"Nonsense Dan, someone needs help – come along man!"

"Well alright, but it sounds funny to me." Dan had just gone behind the tower when Alistair jumped up onto 1462, finding the brake standard, he unwound it until the locomotive began to move, and jumped off the footplate as quickly as he could.

Dan looked back over his shoulder and saw the train moving. "Quick Vicar, quick! They've got us again – I told you there was something fishy!" They reached the track side just as Gordon's van was going by.

"Sam, Sam, what are you doing down there? Quick, get up here." Dan and the Reverend ran after the van, and Gordon and Arthur pulled them aboard, 1462 and her train was now picking up speed. "How are you going to get back?" Gordon asked.

"We can't!" said Sam.

"I'll go" Arthur said "I was on trains during the War, and I've walked along carriage roofs before."

"When they were moving?" Asked Gordon.

"I was told you were a Navy man Mr Chesterford, it's just like being on a swaying deck!"

The Reverend cut in." But we need to be on the footplate, I'm sure Mr Clegg would notice a changed crew – don't you think?"

"It will be alright Sam, when we get to Mallingford I'll nip out and delay him while you and Dan nip round the other side." reassured Gordon.

"I'd better get moving" said Arthur. "She's getting some speed up now."

Arthur climbed up onto the edge of the veranda of the van and put his hands onto the roof, and with Gordon giving him a push, he was on. Once on the roof and crouching low, Arthur got used to the swaying motion and started to move forward. Standing up, he jumped from the van to the carriage, steadied himself and then continued moving along the carriage's roof towards the engine.

They were now passing through open fields and the bright sunlight cast clear shadows onto the passing ground. Mr Clegg was looking down onto his papers spread on the table, something caught Joan's eye, the shadow of someone walking on the carriage roof, and she nudged Mr Blakeworth and indicated to him as unobtrusively as she could the shadow on the field outside.

Just then Mr Clegg made to stand up, to reach for the communication cord. "Err; do you want anything Mr Clegg.?" Mr Blakeworth leant over and being so close prevented Mr Clegg from rising.

"I am going to operate the communication cord Mr Blakeworth, if you don't mind."

"But Mr Clegg, if you do that the brakes and cord will have to be reset before we move again, causing a delay."

"Surely Mr Blakeworth, you know I must carry out a full inspection, including, emergency methods."

"Oh, very well then." Mr Blakeworth moved back, Joan had just nudged him after she had seen the shadow reach the engine.

"Now ladies and gentlemen, I am going to pull the communication cord." So saying he reached across into the cord recess, and pulled. The cord or chain as it actually was, came down and stayed hanging slack. The vacuum of the train brake was destroyed by this action, putting the brakes on, and 1462 squealed to a halt just as Arthur dropped onto the footplate.

Gordon climbed up into the carriage. "Who pulled the cord?" He said looking straight at Mr Clegg.

"All seems in order – you may start the train." Mr Clegg sat back in his seat.

Gordon gave him a look and moved to the carriage door. The indicator at the back of the carriage was standing vertical, so Gordon reached up and turned it back to its horizontal position, restoring the vacuum and the chain returned to its original position.

Up on the footplate Harry woke up as Arthur was sorting out the controls. 1462 now stood quietly hissing, ready to set off again, and Arthur looked back along the train to see if Dan and the Reverend were coming.

Meanwhile back in the van Dan had a thought "Why don't we get back to the engine while the Squire's sorting out that inspector?"

"Good idea Dan, let's get up there now before Gordon gets back." So saying, they dropped down on to the trackside and crept towards 1462.

Seeing this from the footplate, Arthur and Harry quickly climbed down and made their way back to the van, they exchanging knowing winks with each other as they passed. Gordon clambered back up into his van, exchanging glances with his new passengers he blew his whistle and waved his flag – the train set off again.

"Now Mr Chesterford, what's this about Mr Valentine being in Newcastle?"

"Kidnapped!" Gordon said

"Kidnapped – I don't believe it?" Harry exclaimed.

"True enough, all the way to Newcastle, but I'm sure he'll be on his way back to us by now, probably in the comfort of a refreshment coach!"

1462 drew into the branch platform at Mallingford, gently coming to a stand in the customary position. The passengers emerged excited, keen to congratulate the crew of the new locomotive after what they thought had been an uneventful run. Mr Ruddock and Mr Clegg followed, with Mr Blakeworth bringing up the rear.

"Well Mr Clegg, are we fortunate this time?" asked Reverend Weech.

Mr Clegg looked at Sam, noting the sarcasm in his voice. "Well Mr Weech, if you can assure me that this standard of rolling stock will be used regularly, and is not just a borrowed "one off", then I will not withdraw the order Everything is in order and I wish you all good luck for the future."

The gathered crowd cheered, and just as before the locomotive crews of mainline locomotives sensed their success and blew their whistles in salute. Amidst the resulting cacophony of noise Dan clapped the Reverend Weech on the back, who looking heavenwards and smiling apologetically reached across and sounded 1462's whistle in unison.

After the train had returned to Titfield and the Ministry inspectors had bade farewell, they all repaired to The Grasshopper and the celebrations went on until long after closing time.

Harry had been nervous all day; he knew he must now tell Joan of his earlier treachery towards the railway. The Squire and Reverend Weech sensed his unease. "Go on Harry, you won't be happy until you have put this behind you, go outside now and we will send Joan out to you."

Reverend Weech gently moved Harry towards the door, he called to Joan. "Joan! Joan my dear, Harry would like to speak to you outside – please could you go and see him now." As Joan passed him he spoke quietly to her, "Joan, we are behind Harry one hundred percent, please do not be too hasty."

Harry waited nervously beside Mr Valentine's Rover, parked outside after his return to a hero's welcome a few hours before. With the closing of the door as Joan came outside, the sound of merriment was cut short. "Harry!" called Joan, "What is the matter?" The night was warm and scented and the whole valley was lit by the full moon. Joan sat down on the wooden bench in front of the pub window and Harry came over, sitting beside her.

"Oh, I am so glad to get off my feet; it's been a marvellous day. Seth says he might have to alter the height of the counter to suit Mr Valentine, but then he said he might get used to it…"

Harry butted in, he had to speak. "Joan – I did a bad thing. I wrecked the old train – number 1401…"

"What?" Joan gasped "You did what?"

"Look Joan, I'm sorry, honest I am. I just was mad at everybody, I told the Squire and the Reverend and they have forgiven me – they know how sorry I am. And I saved *Thunderbolt*, and I brought back the new engine…"

"I don't believe it! I don't believe them! Nobody told me – how could you have done it Harry – you knew how much I wanted our railway to succeed!"

"I know Joan and I have done my best to put things right. I have been trying to tell you for days, but I just couldn't find the right moment."

"And you call this the right moment? Harry I was on top of the world tonight, and to think the others knew, and had forgiven you….."

"But they did Joan, they have forgiven me – honest! You are still going to marry me – aren't you Joan?"

"Right now Harry I just don't know…" Joan got up and went back into The Grasshopper.

CHAPTER 15

Wednesday

—

Twenty years later

The hall echoed to the two men's footsteps, the high ceiling, the columns and the polished floors formed a suitable setting for the champions of a bygone age. "There she is, as good as new." Reverend Weech stood leaning on his walking stick, standing beside Mr Valentine. *Thunderbolt* stood on a plinth before them resplendent in her bright paint and polished brass work.

"That she is Sam – just look at her, ah what memories. You know it was just here where we had that meeting, it was a close run thing – young Gordon's speech swung it for us I think, happy days…"

A visitor and his son appeared from the other side of *Thunderbolt*. "Excuse me gentlemen, I couldn't help overhearing, but you sound as if you know something more about her?"

"Know her?" Reverend Weech exclaimed "I used to drive her!"

"To see her is to bring back memories of betrayal, ingenuity, bravery and steadfast dedication." Mr Valentine smiled up at *Thunderbolt*.

"Then you must be…" asked the visitor.

"Yes – two of the founder members of the Titfield line!" they both said proudly.

"But weren't you the first…."

"The first preserved railway? Well not exactly, the narrow gauge Talyllyn in Wales was the very first, but we were the first standard gauge line. But ours is not just a preserved line, it still runs seven days a week, providing a regular service." Reverend Weech looked around him. "We had the inquiry meeting right here in Mallingford Museum."

They talked for a while about Titfield and the *Thunderbolt*. "I am sorry" said Reverend Weech, "but my friend and I are not as sprightly as we once were and I'm afraid we need to sit down." He looked at his watch.

"Oh I am sorry for keeping you gentlemen, but I really wanted to hear your story."

"Well sir, in that case may I suggest that we retire to the hostelry across the way? They serve a fine lunch and a good standard of liquid refreshment!" so saying Mr Valentine turned towards the door. He turned his head slightly back towards them." I was hijacked you know!"

"Kidnapped…" sighed Reverend Weech, as he followed them out.

Swinging the large oak doors closed behind him, he swore he could hear *Thunderbolt* in all her glory – the sound seemed to be everywhere. Upstairs at the top of the building, the curator had just switched on an old tape recorder. His uncle had brought it to his house beside the Titfield line whilst *Thunderbolt* was running and had held the microphone out of the window and captured her sound. He listened to it from time to time, and wondered whether he ought to install it downstairs beside *Thunderbolt* herself – he switched it off. The Reverend Weech stood and listened. "You're getting past it old man" he muttered to himself, and followed the others down the steps and out of the museum.

After a very good lunch, which included a number of glasses of sherry and gin and tonic, the visitor who was called Mr Brown wanted to hear the whole story of Titfield and its railway. Between them, the Reverend Weech and Mr Valentine told the story from the closure until the run with 1462 and the new carriage.

"So what happened to *Thunderbolt*?" Mr Brown asked.

"You saw her in the museum." Mr Valentine replied.

"But the running gear, wasn't there was a problem with the bearings?" asked Mr Brown.

"Luckily Albert Lee managed to get the bearings re-metalled so she was put back into good condition before going back to the museum." replied Reverend Weech.

"But didn't you mention another run? Do tell us about that day too, the last run for *Thunderbolt* – please!" Asked Mr Brown.

Thunderbolt's last day.

"Sam! Are you ready?" Olly Matthews stood resplendent in Bishop's derby and railwayman's bib and brace overalls.

"Coming Olly!" replied Sam, closing the Vicarage door.

"It's a splendid day for it Sam – good of you to invite me."

"Nonsense Olly, you were fireman on the first run, it is only fitting that you should be so on the last."

They walked to the end of the Vicarage drive, already the villagers were making their way to the station and there were calls of "Good morning Vicar" and "Nice morning" as they passed.

Looking to their right down the hill they saw Mr and Mrs Valentine coming out of their gate, Mr Valentine removed his trilby and waved it. "Morning Reverend, a very good morning." They waited until the Valentines reached them, and started walking towards the station together.

"I feel a bit of a fraud, not helping to raise steam this morning." said Reverend Weech.

"Nonsense Padre" Mr Valentine interjected "It is about time you had a lie in."

"I am sure Dan and Harry will have her ready." Put in Olly.

The Reverend Weech looked up into the clear blue sky. "It is a lovely day." There was quite a crowd gathered in the station yard and on the platform, the day had been advertised as *Thunderbolt*'s very last running before she went back to the museum.

"Seth hardly had to do anything in the new buffet." Mr Valentine smiled.

"You know Walter, you put on poor Seth far too much and I don't know why you can't do without a drink, just the same as anyone else."

"My dear, it is tradition, it is expected."

They saw Mr Blakeworth who tipped his bowler to the company. "Grand day for it, just like the day we started all of this off."

They heard *Thunderbolt*'s whistle, followed by 1462's, with a hiss of released steam *Thunderbolt* drew slowly into the station. "Bravo! Bravo!" called Mr Valentine. Mr Blakeworth raised his umbrella in salute to Dan who was driving her. Harry followed in 1462, pulling the carriage and Gordon's van.

"She's not double heading then?" Olly asked.

"No, we are running her light, just ahead of 1462 with the actual train as far as the Junction." Sam put his railway cap firmly onto his head and made ready for the off.

"You ready Sam?" Asked Gordon, "I think that all of our passengers are on board."

"Are you ready Olly?" Sam asked.

"Yes, let's go Sam!" Olly Matthews climbed up on to *Thunderbolt's* footplate.

"Goodbye Emily, goodbye Sally – take care of the place!" Sam waved.

Gordon signalled them away with his flag, and with a short "pip" on her whistle *Thunderbolt* steamed majestically out of Titfield Station for the very last time, to the cheers of the villagers and visitors standing on the platform. Harry gave a blast on 1462's whistle in salute, while Arthur oiled around his locomotive, looking forward to firing for a complete run. A couple of minutes later 1462 and its train pulled out and Mr. Valentine enjoyed his first Gin and Tonic of the day. Although it was a little early he called for drinks all round to mark the occasion.

It was not just a normal run to Mallingford; it was a grand procession, with crowds gathering at every vantage point. The valley had never looked lovelier as both engines steamed down the line, passing the water tower and then the crossing, empty since Arthur had fitted new half shafts and returned to Much Abbot with his transporter – it was another beautiful Titfield day.

As they pulled into Mallingford, the railway brass band struck up with "The Entrance of the Gladiators" and a crowd of railwaymen and well wishers stood cheering and waving.

The Reverend Weech followed by Olly Matthews stepped onto the platform and the Curator of Mallingford Museum stepped forward to shake hands with both of them.

"Here you are Sir, she's all yours again! I want to thank you for loaning her to us in our hour of need, she may now retire with honour after the sterling work she has done for us." The crowd clapped, the band struck up for a second time and the two men shook hands again.

"Well said, Sam!" Said Olly Matthews, Bishop of Wellchester.

Harry's train drew in shortly afterwards, and accompanied by yet another rendition of "Entrance of the Gladiators" the passengers left the train, with everybody congratulating each other and admiring *Thunderbolt*.

"Well, what now Sam.?" Asked Gordon.

"I think I would just like to spend some time with *Thunderbolt* before she goes back to the Museum if you don't mind." Sam looked fondly at the historic locomotive standing in the sunshine.

"Very well Sam, you take as long as you like, we will get 1462 and the train ready to go back." He turned to Olly "Would you like to fire a more modern engine Bishop?"

"Would I…" replied the Bishop "But might it not be a little crowded on the footplate?"

"Oh that's no problem, I'm sure Harry and Dan wouldn't mind joining Mr Valentine in the bar." And so the day unfolded, following their by now familiar routine and with another celebration taking place that night in the Grasshopper.

****

The Reverend Weech and Mr Valentine smiled at each other.

"But what happened to the Pearce brothers?" asked Mr.Brown

"You know my throat feels quite dry…" said Mr Valentine. Mr Brown called for another round of drinks.

"Ah, now after Mr Blakeworth paid Pearce and Crump another visit, they decided that they would plead guilty and they got three years apiece. They were also persuaded not to mention Harry Hawkins' involvement. Remember, we also knew they were behind trying to set *Thunderbolt* alight, allowing a loaded passenger train to run away out of control and threatening Harry Hawkins. The other brothers decided they should remove themselves from the district shortly afterwards and we have not seen them since."

"And don't forget me" Mr Valentine looked at Sam, "I was drugged and kidnapped!"

"Ah yes, Mrs Ely, a young woman and a trip to Newcastle without a ticket…" They exchanged glances.

"Of course Arthur Grout has helped a great deal, he has brought more engines and built a workshop by the crossing, and we have a good selection of rolling stock. 1401 was repaired and we found another three carriages for the line."

"What about Harry Hawkins?" asked Mr Brown. Through the door of the pub came the blast of a train whistle.

"Young Harry." Reverend Weech gestured through the open door.

"Young Harry?"

"Oh, didn't I tell you – Joan was upset for a little while but we all rallied round and she soon saw that Harry was the only one for her."

"So?" asked Mr Brown again.

"Do you know they had hardly been married a year when the twins were born, young Harry and Sally. They named her after Sally who helped us and now young Harry drives for us and Sally has taken over the buffet car from her mother."

"What about Gordon and Dan?" asked the young Brown.

"Dan is getting on a bit now, but we made him a bigger home from a camping coach and he still lives in the station yard. Gordon, as you know, is our Squire and runs the market garden up at the hall, he sometimes still helps out in the guard's van."

"Harry and Joan took over the Grasshopper when Fred retired, and on special occasions they still return to the railway, Harry drives and Joan runs the buffet car."

"And I am still trying to find one of those directors coaches…" said Mr Valentine, draining the last of his drink from his glass.

"You know Walter, talking of the twins, set me to thinking…"

"Ah yes Sam, when they were born – now that was a wild night…."

"A wild night?" Asked Mr Brown.

"Now that's another story." Said Mr Valentine, placing his empty glass on the table.

Acknowledgements

—

The publisher would like to thank Tom for writing such a good story in the first place and then for having such great patience with me afterwards. Thank you also to the various friends who read the story in its early stages and a particular thank you to Massimo Moretti at Studiocanal for looking over the finished manuscript and not putting me off the idea of going ahead.

The original film "The Titfield Thunderbolt" is the property of Studiocanal, along with many other classic British film productions, and they have done a wonderful job of both restoring and promoting the film. They have also made many wonderful photographs and other items from the film available to purchase through their partners Media Storehouse.

About the author

—

I first saw The Titfield Thunderbolt as a sixteen year old apprentice motor mechanic at the Odeon Cinema in 1953, in my home town of South Shields. Then, to me, it was just another good Ealing comedy showing the British at their best.

Some forty years later thanks to video, I rediscovered Titfield and its magic. Tibby Clarke's wonderful story was really only meant to be experienced once, but the more I watched the video, the more I realized the story had many loose ends. This then is my idea as to what happened next to the people and machines of Titfield.

Before attempting to read this story, anyone who is not familiar with the Titfield Thunderbolt should get hold of a copy and absorb its magic before reading on.

Tom Young